Mills & Boon Classics

A chance to read and collect some of the best-loved novels from Mills & Boon – the world's largest publisher of romantic fiction.

Every month, four titles by favourite Mills & Boon authors will be re-published in the *Classics* series.

A list of other titles in the *Classics* series can be found at the end of this book.

Margery Hilton

THE INSHINE GIRL

MILLS & BOON LIMITED
LONDON . TORONTO

First published 1970
Australian copyright 1980
Philippine copyright 1980
Reprinted 1980

© Margery Hilton 1970

ISBN 0 263 73281 9

Set in Baskerville 10 on 12 pt.

*Made and printed in Great Britain by
Richard Clay (The Chaucer Press), Ltd.,
Bungay Suffolk*

CHAPTER ONE

'WELL, we're here.'

'And how!'

Della Lane smiled at her companion's rueful tone and said lightly: 'Not turning chicken already, are you?'

'Of course not!' Venetia attempted a tone equally as unconcerned as that of her friend. 'Except we aren't quite there – yet.'

'We will be very soon. They should be here to meet us any moment now.' Della stared across the rain-blurred airstrip to the opening into the bush where a narrow track disappeared into dense greenness and added: 'If they haven't drowned on the way, that is.'

That possibility had already occurred in all seriousness to Venetia, at least that the welcome mat had bogged down on its way, but she refrained from saying so. She listened to the fusillade on the corrugated tin canopy overhead and watched the expanse of red dust that was rapidly changing to glistening cocoa-coloured mud. And she had thought England was wet!

The slight breeze that had swept the airstrip when they got off the plane half an hour ago had stilled, but not before it had coated herself and Della with a fine film of what now reminded her irresistibly of paprika. She glanced down at her once crisp sparkling self and wondered what on earth had possessed her to wear white. Della, in deep coral pink, had fared much better. African seasoning, she thought wryly. Oh well, she would learn!

A movement outside the other building a short distance away caught her attention. The sole staff of Lake Kar-

5

imba airport was locking up and making obvious preparations to depart.

She said uneasily, 'Della, look. I think he's going. Don't you think we'd better ask him to phone, or something? I mean there's nobody else, and if they don't turn up we'll be stuck.'

Della frowned. 'I don't understand it. Jason said in his last cable we would definitely be met here. That he or one of the others would be waiting for us. I think perhaps we'd better ask that bod to put a check call through for us.' She moved to the edge of the shelter afforded by the canopy and wrinkled her nose at the torrential downpour slashing the strip of ground between the two shanties which constituted the airport offices. 'Who's going to brave it?'

'I will.' Suddenly Venetia decided that getting drenched was preferable to being left on a deserted airstrip in the heart of the Kawali bush without knowing what was going to happen next. Anything might have prevented their being met, she thought as she squelched through the mud, heedless now of its effect on her dainty white sandals. The truck or car could have had a puncture or broken down or anything. She neared the other building and the tall African had seen her approach. He ploughed towards her, rain streaming off his waterproof.

'Please,' she said breathlessly, 'no one has come. Is there a phone we could use, or—' she had another idea '. . . is there anywhere around here where we could hire a car? We—'

'No, you wait.' He shook his head earnestly. 'Already I report your arrival. Mr. Kinlay say you to wait. He sending somebody.'

'But when?' she cried. 'Supposing he doesn't?-We might be stuck here for ages. Isn't there a phone we could use?'

'Airport closed now.'

'Closed?' She fell back a pace. 'But phones don't close down.'

'It is rule,' he said imperturbably. 'Phone only for official airport business. Closed when airport closed.'

Officialdom! Venetia closed her eyes. Was there anywhere on the globe where red tape had not reached? 'When is the airport open again?'

'For next plane due in. Friday, nineteen-thirty hours.'

Friday! Three days away!

'What's on fire?' asked Della, having decided to brave the torrent to see what success, if any, Venetia was having. From under a gauzy white scarf, which inadequate protection now resembled transparent wisps of tissue paper on her hair, she looked inquiringly from her young companion to the African's worried expression.

He was betraying signs of restlessness. He had completed his round of duties, strictly according to the regulations, and obviously he didn't care to hang around savouring the harbinger of the rainy season any more than did the two passengers whose formalities he had already attended to, again strictly in accordance with the regulations and the instructions received from Mr. Jason Kinlay. However, he was not entirely without sympathy for their temporary inconvenience. He gave a smile which was very white and intended to be consoling. 'You shelter from wet over there, where I leave open for you, and wait like Mr. Kinlay say. He not be long.' He gestured towards the tin shanty and with a nod hunched his shoulders against the elements and squelched off across the field of red mud.

Venetia and Della looked at one another, and now Della's usually serene features held traces of concern. She said slowly: 'There's obviously been a hold-up. I wonder . . . Could we walk it? Jason said it was only about four miles from the airstrip. The rain's stopping now, and we're so wet it couldn't make much difference if it didn't. Are you game?'

'If you think it would be best. We might be here for hours.' But there was doubt in Venetia's voice, then her glance went to the little pile of luggage visible within the doorway of the hut and was intercepted by Della. The older girl said quickly: 'We can't lug *that*. Let's try and catch the bod and ask him to lock it up till the transport comes. He can't have got far.'

'I'll go.' Venetia was already running fleetly across the airstrip in the wake of the African who had just passed out of sight at the far side. She slowed as she neared the place where the track cut into the green, stickily conscious that athletic antics and Kawali's climate didn't exactly complement each other, and took a deep breath as she passed into the shadowy dimness of the forest. There was a bend ahead around which the African was disappearing and she instinctively cast a glance over her shoulder, half prepared to see the entrance vanish and the trees close about her. The thorn acacias with their pale boles were strangely eerie and the rampant creeper coiled and climbed sinuously everywhere. It was a heavy, unfamilar atmosphere, dark and oppressive, and she shouted, suddenly timorous, and hurried forward, repeating her urgent shout. Then she started with fright as a roaring sound and a swish grew in crescendo. Before her reflexes translated the noise a blaring klaxon sent her springing back over the ruts towards the safety of the side of the track.

A Land Rover swept round the bend and stotted to a halt in a spray of mud. The heads of the two occupants swivelled, two pairs of eyes stared at Venetia's mud-adorned form and two mouths parted with astonishment.

Then the one under the mop of fair curly hair spread slowly into a long grin. Its owner turned to his companion and exclaimed:

'Gee, even the birds of paradise go trekking these days. Or are you hitching, honey?'

He leaned over the side and waved a cheerful salute. 'Hiya, honey. Looking for us?'

Venetia advanced slowly and looked up into one of the most engaging and attractive sets of male features she'd ever set eyes on. A laughing, well-shaped mouth revealed very white teeth, with just enough trace of unevenness to be endearing. Blue eyes crinkled at the corners and seemed even bluer against the tan that heightened the effect of the sun-bleached glints of thick springing hair.

She ventured a smile. 'Are you from Noyali? From Mr. Kinlay at base H.Q. of—'

'Say no more!' Welcoming hands reached out with an embracing gesture. 'You're among friends. You must be our new personnel. Right?'

'Right.' Her smile was curving now.

'And such gorgeous personnel! My, but you're beautiful! I take back everything I said about the old man and *his* luck in having his—'

'Skip it, Johnny.' The cold curt tones of the other man cut into the hot humid air like a breath of frost. 'Where's the other one?'

For the first time Venetia took notice of the man behind the wheel, and the shy warmth of response invoked by Johnny ebbed away as she met an unsmiling glance.

If Johnny had the most attractive features she'd ever seen this man had the coldest. She saw clear grey eyes, made penetratingly direct by a fringing of black lashes under strong, well defined brows, a deep widow's peak from which dark hair sprang back cleanly, making no

9

concession to the carelessness of the current mode, a mouth that was firm and well-shaped and not a little intimidating, and a chin that was uncompromisingly square. He ran that cool glance over her again and said abruptly: 'You're not alone, surely? There's supposed to be two of you.'

The glance said plainly: a kid like you! and she flushed. 'No. Della is back there,' she pointed, 'with the kit. We – that is – I was trying to catch up with the airport man – the controller, or whatever he is – to ask him to keep our luggage. We thought you weren't coming. We were going to walk to the base.'

'Walk!' The dark man raised despairing brows, and Johnny gave a hoot of laughter. 'In that gear?' He looked over her once dainty white attire and laughed again. 'How far do you think you'd have got, my lovely?' He turned to his companion. 'Did you hear the bit about an airport controller? I must remember to tell M'Tambi that! He'll grow another stripe.'

The dark man did not smile. He gestured impatiently to Venetia and said: 'You'd better get in. We'll be bogged down if we stay in this furrow much longer. Come on,' he put out his hand as he spoke and she almost gasped at the iron in the grip that bit into her arm as he helped her into the Land Rover. Surreptitiously she rubbed at the damp sleeve of her jacket and took a deep breath as the vehicle started off with a jolt. For a welcome after a journey of nearly four thousand miles she didn't think much of it! However, Johnny turned suddenly and gave her a warm, reassuring grin and a cheeky thumbs-up gesture, and some of her assurance returned; *he* was nice, anyway.

The airstrip opened before them and Della came into view, the rather anxious expression on her face giving way to a thankful smile as she saw them and waved gaily. When the vehicle nosed alongside the hut she bestowed one of her special smiles impartially on the two men and said brightly: 'Our rescue party – hurrah! We thought you'd got lost.' Her glance flickered to Venetia, then to Johnny. 'Well, who's who?' she asked, arching elegant brows.

Venetia opened her mouth at the same time as Johnny, but the other man spoke first, swinging lithely out of the Land Rover and extending his hand to Della.

He said, 'I'm Simon Manville. This is Johnny Slade. And you . . .?'

Della's small, olive-toned hand rested lightly in his clasp while she calmly made her own lightning assessment, perfectly composed under the keen surveillance of Simon Manville. 'Della Lane, personal assistant to Mr. Kinlay,' she said in her crisp yet musical voice, 'and you've already met Miss Craig – did you introduce yourself, Venetia? And now,' her mouth curved appealingly, 'we're just longing for a glimpse of civilization again – or the nearest you have to it.'

'It depends what you're expecting.' Simon Manville began to stow their kit into the back of the Land Rover.

'A cup of tea, I expect.' Johnny pretended to stagger as he picked up Della's big case. 'How much excess did this cost you?'

'Ssh,' Della smiled, 'the company paid. Thank you.' She accepted his gallant assistance in ensconcing her as comfortably as possible in the Land Rover, while Venetia, wondering why on earth she'd bothered getting out, climbed in again unaided and sat at Della's side. She watched Simon Manville take his place at the wheel and wondered inconsequently just what it was that Della had. He had almost – but not quite – melted into the admiring male deference Della invariably inspired, and it wouldn't be long before the thaw set in completely. It might be quite amusing when it did, Venetia thought with certain satisfaction, still smarting from his brusque treatment of herself. After all, she had got this job on her own merits; he didn't have to look her over as though she were the new kid just out, and wet behind the ears into the bargain. Even Della had had Jason's influence to thank for her transfer from England. Jason had already spent two years on the big hydro-electric installation on Lake Karimba and had finally, after a succession of male personal assistants, none of whom had matched up to his idea of competence, demanded that Della be allowed to join him until the completion of the contract. Somewhat doubtfully Authority had agreed to relax its ban on female personnel, provided they remained at the base H.Q. at Lake Karimba, some seven miles from the site of the great dam being constructed at the mouth of the Nykuni valley.

Della had been jubilant. She adored travel and she was first a career girl. The fact that Jason had missed her and had used considerable string pulling power to gain his own way had elated her immensely. He wanted her, which proved she was almost, if not completely indispensable. Also, she had disliked intensely the new man for whom she had to work during Jason's absence.

The great news had started strange yearnings and restlessness in Venetia. She had shared a flat with Della, daughter of her mother's closest friend, for nearly two years, and although there was five years' difference in their ages the two girls got along together extremely well. Of course anyone would get on well with Della. There was something about her serene, good-humoured personality that deflected quarrelsome impulses, and she was also extremely perceptive. It was not long before she had drawn from her youthful flatmate the long-held dream of faraway places, the wistful longing to spread youthful wings and fly, and perceived the invisible barrier that a sheltered upbringing had built. For Venetia's mother had died when Venetia was only eight, and her father, a brilliant research chemist, had bound his only child to him with loving if misguided bonds of protection, until suddenly, just after Venetia's sixteenth birthday, he had met and married a newcomer to his department who was not many years older than Venetia herself. At last Venetia was free.

Her new young stepmother opened the gates to freedom and Della had shown the way. The knowledge she had been unable to help absorbing through the years of closeness to her father and his work now proved unexpectedly valuable, and she experienced no difficulty in gaining a secretarial post with the chief analyst in the department of agricultural research attached to the company for which Della worked. And then Della's great moment had arrived. The building of the new hydro-electric installation, for which the company had gained the tender, was also entailing a resettlement scheme and with it new opportunities for the adventurous and the travel-thirsty. Apart from the engineers, the irrigation specialists and the many allied experts such a vast scheme necessitated, someone had to look after the enormous outpourings of paperwork in triplicate and quadruplicate without which no official undertaking was complete in the twentieth century. It was here that Venetia's qualifications stood her in good stead. Authority had bowed to Jason Kinley's wish and the appointment of a woman medic who specialized in tropical medicine rapidly followed Della's transfer, and Venetia, to her great joy, found her application successful. Now, a stringent medical and a battery of inoculations behind her, she was on her way to the heart of Africa, to discovery and a new freedom with Della.

So occupied was she with retrospect she did not notice that the dense green latticework overhead was thinning and brilliant sunshine evaporating the moisture into rising mist from the waterlogged earth. Then Della nudged her and pointed.

They were emerging from the forest and the lake had come into view beyond a wide, gently undulating stretch of open country. The hills rose, tree-girded and mist-wreathed, at the far side of the water and vivid gold sun-rays were piercing the distant rainclouds and scattering liquid brilliants across the calm surface.

Della shaded her eyes and murmured, 'It's beautiful. Oh, look at those birds! Aren't they heavenly?'

'Flamingoes,' said Johnny.

But Della's excited gaze had already left the graceful rose-down birds and spotted other brilliant splashes of colour.

'See those butterflies, Venetia? Over those yellow flowers. Surely they're too enormous to be real.'

Johnny smiled indulgently at the raptures and Simon Manville said dryly: 'We're not very well up in lepidoptera, I'm afraid, but they're genuine all right.'

Venetia said nothing, her attention shifting constantly over a vista that held a promise and beauty at once exciting and not a little awe-inspiring. Presently it returned to the sparkling waters of the lake and she sighed, suddenly conscious of the hot sticky state of herself and a temperature which was going to take some time to become acclimatized to. She murmured dreamily: 'Just take me to that water and drop me in.'

'I doubt if you'd thank us if we did,' said Simon Manville over his shoulder.

'It isn't safe for swimming?' queried Della.

'Its inhabitants aren't exactly friendly,' Johnny grinned, and pulled a fearsome grimace of dread. Della laughed, but Simon Manville's profile remained set and unsmiling.

He said, 'Bathing in the lake is out, and just remember that, both of you.'

Della's expression remained unconcerned, but Venetia's mood of enchantment had been abruptly dispelled. He sounded as though he thought we were a couple of empty-headed kids, she thought resentfully, as though we hadn't been through all the reminders of the dangers that could lurk for the careless behind the colourful exotic face of the tropics. Hadn't they been warned? leeches, snakes, ticks, prickly heat, dehydration; no bare feet – jiggers, no forgetting paludrine – the mosquito had not been completely suppressed in Kawali, remember water discipline, watch out for ... don't ... The list had seemed endless. Venetia sighed; she had the feeling that she at least was going to be on the receiving end of them all over again – and a few more no one else had thought of!

*   *   *

The base camp lay above a long gentle incline rising some two miles from the north-western shore of the lake. Venetia, who had vaguely expected something on the austere lines of an army encampment, was pleasantly surprised to see the neat row of prefabricated buildings which housed the administrative offices and even more delighted when the Land Rover rolled on past them and reached the little white bungalows behind cool green lawns which were obviously the quarters of the personnel.

A short, thickset man of about forty wearing the same faded kind of bush shirt and slacks as the two men appeared on the verandah of the first and largest bungalow. He must have been waiting for the sound of the vehicle, for he came to the white gate as it halted and seized Della's hands to help her out, smiling broadly and bestowing a fatherly kiss on her cheek. It was plain he was delighted to see her.

Della made introductions, as although Venetia knew the great Jason Kinlay by sight to him she would be only one of the army of employees in the vast building back home. But his greeting was none the less friendly and Venetia decided instantly that she liked him. Lucky Della, she thought, to have no cause for apprehension over what her boss was going to be like to work for. That was something Venetia had yet to face, and responding to Jason's benignity she sent up a small prayer that she would fare as well as her friend.

'Now what would you like first?' inquired Jason, tucking a friendly hand under each girl's arm and moving towards the bungalow. 'A cup of tea, or a shower, or a look at your own quarters? They're all ready for you.'

'All three together,' said Della, and he laughed. 'I suggest you come and have tea with me first and cool down. Johnny can take your kit over there for you, then you can go and make yourselves at home. You're sharing a bungalow, by the way,' his brown eyes glanced at each girl in turn, 'I thought you'd want to be together, seeing you're friends. Okay?'

'Perfect,' said Della, following Venetia through the door he indicated and sighing at the coolness of an air-conditioned lounge. 'My, they've done you well, Jason,' she remarked, with the easy familiarity of a favoured colleague. 'Quite a little home from home.'

A white-coated boy came silently, and when Jason had ordered tea Della asked, 'How is everything going?'

'So-so,' he said. 'We're about two months behind schedule, but it could have been worse, considering all.

We got the labour dispute settled, thank God. Why that fool Dyson brought in the Myenga workers I'll never fathom. He knows the Oskiri have been gunning for them for years – centuries!' he added impatiently, and sighed. 'That's just another headache we have to face when we flood the valley. It's all very well for the planners in their corridors of power to ordain: "Resettle them." How do you shift an entire village from a valley they've lived in and died in for centuries?' He swore softly. 'Tell them they'll have better soil, better irrigation, no more bilharzia and no more protein deficiency? They'll settle to keep their village, and their bilharzia and malnutrition.'

Della murmured sympathetically and plied more knowledgeable questions to which Jason enlarged at length, seeming grateful for a fresh ear of sympathy and understanding into which to air the many problems his considerable responsibility had brought him.

Venetia listened idly, content to relax and enjoy the tea and biscuits the houseboy brought and let her gaze explore the colourful garden fronting the bungalow. She had been secretly relieved to hear that she was sharing quarters with Della; first nights alone in strange surroundings still spelled a slightly uneasy restlessness for her, and she had never been in so alien a surrounding as this one. Presently she heard Della say lightly:

'And how's Claire?'

Jason put a hand up before his face and shook it slightly, his expression partly resigned, partly humorous, and Della smiled faintly with understanding and stood up, glancing at Venetia.

Jason also got to his feet. 'Yes, I expect you'll be anxious to start settling in. I'll run you along.'

The bungalow allotted to the two girls was only about five hundred yards away and when Della protested that they could walk Jason brushed aside her protest. 'You've had a long and tiring journey, besides, you'll have to learn to conserve your energy here. The tropics can have an enervating effect when you've just come out.' His shrewd glance was on Venetia as he spoke, noting the tenseness of suppressed weariness in her small, fine-boned features and the delicate skin touched with a heat flush of transparent rose. 'I should rest this evening,' he went on. 'Don't start your reorganizing exertions straight away. You'll have all day tomorrow for that.'

'What! No work?' exclaimed Della.

'Not tomorrow. Take a day or two to settle in and get over the journey.' He slowed the big Citroen to a halt and smiled. 'Here we are. See you both for dinner tomorrow evening, if not before, and I'll introduce you round. Claire should be back tomorrow afternoon. Cheerio!'

A friendly wave and he drove off, leaving Venetia and Della to walk slowly up the straight red path to their new domain.

It was smaller than Jason's but quite big enough for them, Venetia decided, following Della on the first tour of inspection. There was a wide verandah, on to which broad screens opened from the living-room. There were two bedrooms, a small but well-equipped kitchenette with a cooker, an icebox and a breakfast area, and there was a shower room next door to it. There was also a house-boy, whose name, he informed them, was Tobi, and his first request disconcerted Della for once in her calm, competent life. What did they want for the evening menu?

After a pause Della said helplessly, 'Oh, anything. Just let yourself go, Tobi,' and the boy grinned, then seeing that apparently nothing else was demanded of him promptly disappeared.

'I shall have to get used to this,' Della giggled. 'I think

you'd better take over the domestic management – you're better at it than me.'

'Oh, yes? What makes you think I'll be any better?' Venetia surveyed the pile of luggage stacked in the hall and then walked into one of the bedrooms. 'Which room do you want?'

'Either,' said Della, 'they're both exactly the same.' She gazed round the bare little room about which the odour of paint still lingered and observed wryly, 'We just can't escape from the institute. Cream paint and cream wash or whatever it is all the way through. No imagination. And iron cots!' She plumped down experimentally to test the bed's softness and looked at the screened windows. 'They might have given us some curtains. Open them, Ven, please and let a bit more air in. I can smell creosote. I expect it's been daubed around to discourage the ants.'

'We could make our own curtains,' said Venetia, opening the screens and inspecting the shutters outside. 'Are we supposed to close these as well at night?'

Della shrugged. 'Don't ask me. If it's stormy, I suppose, or cold.'

'Is it ever cold here?' It was more of an exclamation than a question as Venetia flapped her hand in front of her hot face.

'I doubt it.' Della stretched herself out full length on the bed and said lazily, 'I'm just as much a raw recruit as you are.' She closed her eyes. 'But we'll learn.'

'Yes.' Venetia had no doubt of it. She stared at the dark mysterious hills at the far side of the valley. The sun had gone now and the lake lay limpid, a deep rose and blue-streaked mirror crested by the forest cladding the hills. The scene held a strange brooding quality, and she shifted her gaze to the immediate vista before her. The garden had been laid out attractively round a central lawn, and she remembered with thankfulness Jason telling them that all the gardens were tended by a communal staff; just as well; neither she nor Della had a clue about gardening – and here! She smiled a little at the thought, her eyes appreciating a large cluster of graceful, waxen white flowers below the verandah's edge. Before her they were visibly closing their petals and drooping, quivering like bells as the vibrations of sound ceased, and a misted violet tinge glowed in the whiteness. She sad suddenly, 'Look, Della. It's dark. Quite dark, except for those big pink feathers in the sky over there.'

'Why don't you lie down?'

'I'm not tired now. Della . . .'

'What?'

'Could we go out? It's cooler now.'

'I haven't got the strength. But you go, if you feel like a wander. Don't get lost, will you?'

'No.' Venetia moved.

'And shut the screens behind you! We'll have all the nightlife in.'

Obediently Venetia closed the screens behind her. She stood for a moment, savouring the small throb of expectancy that ran through her as she looked over the threshold of her first African night. From being a small girl she had always hugged to herself a delicious love of exploring new places. Holidays with her father had invariably begun with his exhausted grumble when they were on their first tour of exploration: 'I'm not going round one more corner – even if the end of the rainbow's there,' and back they would go, back round all the corners she hadn't been able to resist. 'Just round this one – to see.' But no next corner in the past had ever held the promise that might lie round the next one in Africa.

Soundlessly she let herself out of the white gate and looked left and right. To the left stretched the row of bungalows, wide spaced, the friendly glow of lanterns strung like giant glow-worms above garden gates and verandahs, and from rooms unseen came voices, a ring of deep laughter, a chinking of glasses, disembodied sounds on the still air.

That was the way they had come in Jason's Citroen. She would turn right, past the long low building that had been pointed out to them as the dispensary.

Her sandalled feet noiseless on the hard-beaten red road, she strolled along towards the white building and the darkness beyond. What was it going to be like working for six months in a practically all-male province? Della had chuckled about being the first feminine invaders, but after all there was Claire, Jason's wife, who had flown out the previous week. Venetia had not met her, but she knew she was considerably younger than Jason and it had been common conjecture as to how long Claire would stick it before the climate and the lack of social life sent her screaming back to London and her gay little coterie. Della had been non-committal on the subject, but Venetia had not been able to help reflecting that if she had been in Claire's shoes she would not have wanted to be parted from her husband all that length of time. It didn't seem natural, Venetia thought, and for the second time the surmise she had not liked to mention to Della occurred to her; had Della's transfer to rejoin Jason had anything to do with Claire's decision to fly out to her husband?

Loyalty to her friend would not allow her to speculate on this question and she pushed it out of her mind as her steps brought her abreast of the dispensary. There was a light in one of the windows and she paused for a few moments, her thoughts turning to Doctor Muriel Vanders, the base's M.O. What would she be like? Old, young, friendly or . . .?

The light flicked out suddenly and Venetia moved on; she would meet Dr. Vanders and everyone else soon enough. Meanwhile, should she turn back? There were no more buildings or lights. This was the end of the settle ment. The road came to an end and narrowed abruptly into what looked like a footpath that began to drop and twist among bushes and the first scattering of trees before the forest looming a little way further on.

Probably Venetia would have turned back then if she had not heard the musical rush of a stream and seen the myriad traceries of a cloud of fireflies. The will-o'-the-wisp of African magic drew her footsteps on to the path, down its rough twists and turns, and filled her nostrils with the rich odours of earth and the prodigality of tropical growth.

Suddenly she came on the stream. It cut deeply under the path, spanned by a narrow rickety bridge that creaked scarily as she stepped on it. A single rough batten was the only guard rail on one side and she rested her hands on it, listening to the dark waters bubbling below amid a tangle of creeper and coiling roots. The fireflies still danced like golden sparks and above the sky was like a great black velvet pincushion pricked with stars.

A sigh of sheer content escaped her. All her former tiredness had gone. This was one of those wondrous moments when time stood still, capturing and holding the magic. She stood very still; the slightest movement would destroy the enchantment. Then a showering spark hissed in the water and a shadow detached itself on the path. Venetia's hands clenched on the rail and she froze.

'Trying to get high on beauty?'

The planks gave ominously beneath her feet and two

22

hands came to rest on the rail alongside her own. The voice said: 'Never heard that beauty can be deadly?'

Slowly she turned her head and looked into the shadowy features of Simon Manville. Painful relief flowed through her and she said defensively: 'I just came out for some air, and to – to walk a little. Is there anything wrong with that?'

'No,' he said laconically, 'if you can cope.'

'Well, I'm not lost.'

'No, not yet. But you're scared stiff.'

'I am not!' Her head went up proudly.

'Then why did you jump like a scalded cat when I spoke to you?'

'What do you expect if you come creeping up out of the dark like that?'

'I'd expect a little more sense. Look.' A torch flashed on in his hand and the beam focused and came to rest on something coiled amid a tangle of roots just below the bridge. She saw the twin winking rubies and the slow sinuous uncoiling, then the snake slid away under the tangle, out of sight.

He switched off the torch and said, 'That's what I mean. It happened to be harmless, but it mightn't have been. Find your feet first – in daylight, Miss Craig. Come on, I'll take you back.'

Somewhat chastened, she turned obediently and followed the small dancing circle of the flashlight. Simon Manville's steps were long and firm, one to every two of hers, and suddenly she felt resentment of the way he had spoken. His friend – if Johnny were his friend – wouldn't have been so beastly and sarky, even if the place was crawling with snakes. Anyway, he'd said it was harmless, and but for him she'd never have seen it, nor it her. And of course she'd been startled when he appeared, creeping up on her like that.

Silently he escorted her back to the bungalow, and now all the magic of discovery had flown. At the gate he stopped, gave a brief inclination of his head and bade her good night. She returned it brusquely and was about to pass through when he checked her abruptly.

'Don't make a habit of wandering around outside the limits of the base at night, or do anything else silly like flinging your screens wide open at night when you feel there isn't a breath of air in the place. You won't get any more fresh air, but you will get bitten.'

Venetia drew a deep, fuming breath. 'Thank you, Mr. Manville, for the advice; however, I've already had it. Good night!' She pushed at the gate and almost ran up the path and into the bungalow.

She found Della lounging in a rattan chair, a book in her hand and a tall glass in the other. There was also the lingering trace of a smile round her lips. She glanced up at Venetia's flushed, furious face and arched her brows. 'Whatever happened to you?'

'What happened!' Venetia wanted to have something to fling down. Without either bag or gloves or jacket she lacked this simple form of escape valve. Giving a frustrated gesture she turned back and found slight relief in slamming the door. 'That man!'

'What man, darling?'

'Simon Manville! Talking to me as though I were still wet behind the ears and an imbecile into the bargain. I'd just found a most heavenly little spot to cool off and it was such a gorgeous night, and then *he* landed in it.' She paused for breath after this stormy account and dropped into a chair. 'Obviously he's going to be one of those real bossy pests, spying on us all the time and snooping around in that sarky way of his.'

'Well, he *is* the senior settlement officer. He'd only be thinking of your welfare.' Della sipped her drink. 'I rather like protective men.'

'Protective! This one's a walking book of Queen's Regulations! That's what my father would call him.'

'Have a drink and cool down, love,' Della advised, 'and forget him.'

'Yes, if he lets me.' Venetia got up and went to the tray near Della's chair. It held a muslin-covered jug of fruit juice, a couple of bottles and a thermal container of ice. 'This looks nice. I've a thirst to empty that lake.' She saw the other used glass and glanced at her friend. 'Don't tell me you've started on the hard stuff already? You know what they told us.'

Della shook her head. 'Not guilty. I've had a visitor.'

'Jason?'

'No.' Della smiled teasingly.

'Well, it couldn't have been His Highness – he was too busy playing policeman and you're looking too pleased with yourself.' Suddenly she realized the visitor could only have been . . . 'Oh, no!' she wailed. 'Was it Johnny?'

'It was.'

'And I had to miss him! You have all the luck.' Venetia subsided into her chair with a sigh. 'He's a dish.'

'Definitely a dish.' Della lit a cigarette and exhaled thoughtfully. 'For a little one you've come out of your shell, miss. Fallen for him?'

'Well . . .' Venetia coloured and took a hasty sip of fruit juice. 'You like him as well, don't try to kid me you don't.'

'True. Remember what we decided before we left home?'

Venetia nodded, watching with wide eyes over the rim of her glass and looking like a child caught out in naughtiness. 'Do you think we should?'

'Why not? As long as we remember falling in love is out. A flirtation for the six months we're going to be here and then a sweet good-bye when it's over. Definitely no involvements.'

Venetia said nothing, and Della observed lightly: 'You're too young and I'm definitely a career girl. But there's no reason why we shouldn't have fun.' She hesitated and wrinkled her nose in a comical grimace. 'Trouble is, it's going to be awkward if we both fancy the same candidate.'

After a moment or so Venetia said, 'Surely he isn't the only one – in a project of this size. *All* men!'

'No,' Della's mouth quirked, 'there's *your* new friend.' She grinned as her young companion shuddered. 'All right, I know! But I quizzed Jason about this important matter while you were daydreaming this afternoon and he said he was afraid we were going to be unlucky. Apart from the crew of engineers working up on the dam itself, and they're in camp on the site, living pretty rough, I gather, the only two likely unattached males who are personable and about the right age are young Johnny and our charming Mr. Manville.'

Venetia digested this and sighed ruefully. 'I suppose it's true, but I can hardly believe it.'

Della nodded. 'But you know, Ven, these silent grim types are often quite a wow if one goes to work on them the right way. Why on earth didn't you try the helpless little girl approach? He'd have been eating out of your hand.'

'I prefer not to try looking any more helpless than I can help,' said Venetia stiffly. 'Anyway, if you think he could be such a wow then why don't you try wowing him yourself?'

26

'I prefer the gay types,' said Della promptly.

'Yes, well, so do I.'

Della sighed. 'To think we imagined hordes of gorgeous, girl-starved men waiting to fight over our favours! What a hope! Of course we could always toss for it.'

Venetia stifled a yawn, conscious of a sudden onslaught of delayed travel weariness. Remembering she hadn't yet unpacked a single thing she decided her overnight bag would have to suffice for one more night and stood up and stretched. 'If you like. But you'll win – you always do.'

'What do you bet me?' Della was rummaging in her bag. 'Heads or tails?'

'Heads – can I spin it?'

'It's my lucky penny, mind.'

'That's what I mean.' Venetia giggled and grabbed the coin, which wasn't a penny but an old silver crown with a hole bored through it which Della sometimes wore on a silver chain.

The older girl watched with amused eyes as Venetia solemnly tried to flip the coin with inexpert fingers. It dropped and rolled and Della pounced with an outstretched toe to check its course. 'It's gone under my chair.' Della leaned sideways, beginning to laugh, and shuffled her chair along without getting out of it. 'Now let it stand, whatever it is, or we'll be on with second tries all night.' She looked at Venetia's kneeling form and added dryly: 'Congrats! It's heads. Good luck.'

Venetia sat back on her heels and the expression on her small face hovered between laughter and apprehension. 'Do you think we should, Della?'

'Why not?' Della tucked the coin back into her bag. 'There won't be much scope for social life around here, so we'll have to make our own recreation, and I guess the oldest kind is still the most fun. Anyway, you're dying to have your first affair, aren't you? Now's your chance. No one to disapprove. We're miles away from dampening relatives and gossipy friends. I say let's enjoy our freedom. Just play it light and keep your head, young Ven.'

'Yes . . .' Venetia looked extremely doubtful. Somehow the gay little idea of six months playing at flirtation which they had giggled over while they were packing to set off no longer seemed so amusing and clever. Now, Venetia knew a sudden doubt as to her ability to wear the mantle of a flirt. Della would carry it off to perfection, but then Della was – Della. Confident, beautiful, never at a loss for exactly the right thing to say and do, whereas . . . She said aloud, 'But what about you? I mean . . .'

Della regarded her with affectionate amusement. 'I promise faithfully to keep well out of Johnny's way and leave you a free hand, if that's what's worrying you.'

'Yes, I know, but it isn't going to be much fun for you if there isn't anyone else. Hadn't we better forget it?'

'Chicken already? Oh, I see.' Light dawned and Della laughed. 'Don't worry about me. There's still the flip side, you know. Even if it's a tough flip side,' she added ruefully.

'Flip side?' A shade of alarm widened Venetia's eyes and she stared at her friend. 'Not . . . you don't mean Jason, surely? He's married.'

'Jason! Good heavens, no!' Della got to her feet and stretched sinuously like a cat. 'Whatever gave you that idea? No, I shall have to hoe the stony trail, and from what you tell me it's going to be quite a challenge.' A musing light glowed in her dark eyes as she put her glass back on the tray. 'Seeing that you've won our fair handsome Johnny it looks as though I've no alternative but to try my luck at wowing our granite-visaged senior settlement officer. Wish me luck, darling.'

Simon Manville! A lean saturnine face swam into Venetia's mental view and she slowly scrambled to her feet, looking at Della's unconcerned smile with apprehensive eyes. 'You'll need it,' she breathed. 'And how!'

CHAPTER TWO

THE first person the girls bumped into the next day was Johnny himself.

After a leisurely breakfast and stern rejoinders to each other that they must finish unpacking Della and Venetia reluctantly ignored the call of the sun and spent the morning disposing of their possessions to appropriate places and making the small touches that transform character-less rooms into individual domains. That done, they felt conscientiously free to embark on a tour of exploration and find the store which Jason had told them was at the other end of the site, near the administration offices.

The skies were brazenly clear, the distant lake a shim-mering glassy pearl, and, as Della observed, it was *hot*!

The briskness of their walk, automatic after a lifetime of Britain's climatic inclemency, slowed the moment they left the shade of the verandah.

'I shall never get used to this,' Della remarked. 'It's taken an entire morning to do an hour's work.' She leaned on the gate, a slim attractive figure in lime green tailored slacks and a cream shirt carelessly open at her throat. Suddenly Venetia felt dissatisfied with her own choice of garb. Her pink dacron dress felt sticky and anything but cool and she hadn't had it on for more than a quarter of an hour. She passed through the gate after Della and sighed; it was her own fault; she'd been warned about man-made fibres, that they weren't as comfortable for tropical wear as natural materials, but the slim slip of pink with white floral sprays patterning it had looked so cool and attractive when she'd tried it on that she hadn't been able to resist it, and the thought of the drip-dry, crease-resisting qualities had weighed automatically in its favour. Well, now she knew! Della's voice recalled her.

'I hope the fair Claire is behaving herself,' she was saying. 'You never met her, did you?'

'No, I'd just joined the department before Jason came out here.'

'Poor Jason,' Della said with feeling. 'She's a bitch. He's had a dog's life with her. I remember once . . .'

Della's recollection was cut short by the swish of tyres and a squeal of brakes.

Johnny Slade leaned out of the runabout and smiled widely. 'Greetings, my lovelies. Where are you bound?' His smiling glance slid from Della to Venetia and back to Della.

Venetia opened her mouth to say: the store, and heard Della say quickly, 'Venetia wants to shop, and I'm going to report to my boss.'

'Hop in.' Johnny ostentatiously flicked his handkerchief over the shabby bench seat at the back and held out his hand to Della. 'You never walk here if you can ride.'

'We must put in an application for transport, then,' said Della.

'And rob me of the pleasure? Now, H.Q. or engineering admin.?' Johnny put on a fine burst of speed that sent the dust swirling at the rear, then whizzed round the turning circle which was exactly centre of the site.

'H.Q., please,' said Della, laughing as she pointed at the neat white building directly opposite and the Citroen parked at the side under an awning, indicating that Jason would not be far away.

'Hold tight.' Johnny solemnly drove across the road and drew to a stop within six inches of the entrance. 'Shall

31

I wait, ma'am?'

'No, you idiot.'

Della got out, laughing, and Johnny gave a mock groan. 'When do I see you again?'

'Not today. I have business. Look after Venetia.'

'Yes, ma'am.' Johnny saluted and watched the trim figure purposefully enter the wide screen doors and disappear behind them without a backward glance. Only then did his gaze swivel. 'Well now, Miss Venetia, and what were you wanting to buy?'

'Curtains.'

'Curtains? You mean those things they hang at windows?'

'Those things they hang at windows,' Venetia repeated solemnly. 'Will I get material in the store here?'

'I doubt it. They just keep stuff like tobacco and shaving gear and the little items poor bachelors far from the comforts of home might run out of. Anyway,' he gave that endearing grin, 'what do you want to shut the view in for?'

'We don't,' she smiled. 'We just want to make our place look like home.'

'Aha, the woman's touch.' Johnny nodded wisely. 'I guess there's another place round here that's sadly in need of the little womanly touches. I always knew something was missing; now I know what it is.'

'Curtains?'

'Not exactly, but now I think of it, those four blank walls I wake up to every morning are pretty deadly. If you would lend your feminine expertise and suggest colours . . . Then I could send a picture home to my mum and let her see that her boy's living in a civilized manner. She's convinced I'm living in a cave in the jungle.'

'Are there any caves in the jungle?'

'I—' Johnny stopped and then hurriedly switched on the motor. 'It's too hot to stay stationary. Let's go.'

'Where?' Venetia had not seen the tall figure of Simon Manville emerging from another building nearby. She pointed. 'Isn't that the store down there?'

'I know a better place,' said Johnny confidently. 'Ever been to a native market?'

'No, this is my first time abroad – real abroad.' She settled back, appreciating the breeze that speed generated against her hot face and preparing to make the most of this unexpected interlude with the engaging Johnny.

'What do you mean by real abroad?'

'Well, somewhere like this.'

'Ah, you mean romantic faraway places. Not fish and chips on the Costa Brava or paper hats in Portugal?'

'Something like that. I think I'm going to need a sun-hat.'

'We'll get one for you, with a bit of luck. You should be wearing sunglasses as well, until you get used to the glare. Might save you a headache.'

'I have some.' She reached into her bag and took out the dark glasses, to exclaim almost immediately after donning them: 'Oh, they spoil the colours. What are those, Johnny?'

He cast a quick glance to where she pointed. 'Those pink starry flowers? Carissa, I think. The ferny stuff is wild asparagus.' He smiled. 'Africa's fecund, to say the least. You'll soon be taking it all for granted.'

'Perhaps.' She did not sound convinced, her wide gaze darting continuously across the blaze of tangled colours amid the green each side of the track, and he smiled again.

'I prefer English peaches and cream any day. The kind I have sitting beside me at this moment.'

His blue eyes danced provokingly and Venetia decided

to wear her sunglasses after all. The colourful scene continued to unwind past her fascinated gaze while the runabout bounced on over the ruts and Johnny whistled a soft, gay little tune. Presently they came to a river, fringed with reeds and dotted with floating saucer-like flowers, which flowed alongside the track for a distance, then the beginning of a banana plantation, briefly skirted, and at last the outskirts of a big sprawling village. Abruptly the track seemed lost in a big, tramped flat clearing, pocked liberally with spring-shattering potholes.

Johnny slowed to circumnavigate a mammy trader who doggedly pushed a two-wheeled cart piled high with a miscellany of market produce. Ancient tyres clad its wheels and three small boys wearing garishly coloured shirts and faded shorts which looked miles too big for them alternately aided the pushing progress and darted to retrieve the occasional casualty that rolled off the over-loaded vehicle into the dust. Scraggy hens and even scraggier dogs of indeterminate breed were a further driving hazard, refusing to move until the runabout was almost on them, and Venetia held her breath when a cow lumbered across, nosed vainly for grazing, and wandered placidly on its way between the clusters of thatched huts which reminded Venetia irresistibly of enormous squat mushrooms wearing coolie hats.

'We'll have to park the jalopy here and walk,' said Johnny. 'Okay?'

'Okay.' She climbed out excitedly, almost before he halted under the shade of a wide-branched tree.

'Hey! Slow down.' Johnny linked a casual arm within hers and restrained her impetuous haste as they mingled with the crowd moving sluggishly down the space between the stalls and the tiny separate territories of those vendors who possessed no stall but the square of earth on which they laid out their wares.

Firmly he drew her past the calabash carver, away from the man in the white robe with the crocodile skins, the woman fashioning big fly whisks, and the ominous fascination of the ju-ju stall.

'A hat,' said Johnny, 'before I have to carry you back with sunstroke.'

'But they've discarded the old theory about wearing hats. Topees are old hat these days.'

'Don't you kid yourself. This is where the danger lies.' Johnny's fingers brushed over the nape of her neck and she suppressed the flutter his touch caused. 'Here we are.'

The haberdashery stall was one of the largest in the market, with a big shady awning under which Venetia thankfully moved and pushed the tendrils of hair back from her heated face.

'Hats over here,' said Johnny. 'Those are baskets,' drawing her away from the cluster of woven straw baskets which had caught her attention. 'Not that they look much different,' he added, running a critical glance over the hats and then over her. 'How about this little number?' He plonked a gay-hued effort with a wide brim on her head and stood back, considering.

'I'd like one of those, I think.' She pointed. 'The ones like the coolie kind.'

Altogether it was a wonderful afternoon, filled with laughter and light-hearted banter, and Johnny was the most beguiling companion. With him she dithered over the choice of curtain material, giggled over the gaily coloured print they eventually chose and admired as he bargained expertly for her and added a small wood carving in the form of a paper knife bound with fine wire which caught her fancy.

At last they strolled back to the runabout, Johnny cheerfully balancing the unwrapped bale of material on his head, and Venetia, hot, tired and dusty but happy, carrying her sundry purchases in one of the native baskets.

'I don't know what you're going to do with that,' he remarked as he stowed it on the back seat.

'Go shopping again, of course. Besides, I need something to tote my odds and ends about in, if we go bathing or picnicking anywhere,' she added vaguely.

'We'll have to arrange something.' He put the vehicle into motion. 'Just let us know the moment you get your working hours settled and know your free time.'

'What do you do? Your job, I mean?' she asked shyly.

'Me?' he grinned. 'In between loafing around I'm an agricultural chemist – if that means anything to you.'

'It does. You analyse soil samples for deficiencies, mineral content and so on. Assess the worth of fertilizers in differing soils, and advise on crop rotation and—'

'Hey! Are you trying to brief me?'

'No,' she smiled demurely. 'I've been doing secretarial assistant along that line.'

'And can you spell?'

'I think so.'

'Does this mean I don't have to type out my own reports any more?'

'It does.'

'Whoopee! I've three waiting to be done. When do you start?'

'As soon as you want me to – sir!'

'Oh, you darling!' Johnny leaned sideways, aimed a kiss which caught her somewhere between her mouth and her chin, and the runabout swerved ominously.

'Look out!' she squealed.

He laughed. 'Your hat got in the way.'

'Ahem, I think you'd better use both hands as well –

for driving.' She leaned back and drew down the big floppy brim of her hat to partly conceal the colour in her cheeks, and a small smile quirked Johnny's mouth as he withdrew the steadying arm he had whipped round her when the vehicle lurched.

She wasn't sure what brought Simon Manville into her mind at that moment, but come he did, and had the effect of sobering down a slight feeling of breathlessness. She couldn't help wondering what the afternoon would have been like in *his* company. There'd have been no laughter, no bartering, no joyous teasing and no wonderful feeling as though she had known him all her life. Probably a series of do's and don'ts, she reflected, and sarky rejoinders. In fact, with the redoubtable Mr. Manville it was unlikely that the afternoon would have happened at all.

The site was deserted when the runabout rolled back along the red road at sundown. Johnny helped her out, carried her shopping into the little hallway, and then clicked his heels together as he gave a comical little salute.

'You'll be along at the Kinlays' tonight?'

She nodded, eyes glowing.

'I'll see you then. So long, Brighteyes.'

She remained there a few moments, watching his lithe form swing down the path and vault into the runabout, then she wandered indoors, unaware of the glow lingering about her and not seeing Della emerge from the shower and lean back against the door to watch. Then she saw her and stopped.

'Well, well!' Della left the door to support itself and straightened, thrusting her hands into the pockets of her short terry robe. 'So you got back. Had a good time?'

'Super!'

'Ye-e-s,' Della drawled, and upturned her glance. 'I

can see pie in the sky all right. Take a pair of sparkling eyes ...' she trilled, waltzing into the bedroom and striking an ecstatic pose in front of the mirror, 'someone's crossed the rubicon ...' she spun round. 'Come on, give!'

'We went to the market at – I don't even know the name of the place – it was miles away, though.' Venetia wandered to the mirror and inspected her reflection under the hat. 'Johnny did tell me the name. It sounded something like—'

'Does it matter? For goodness' sake take it off. Little Eva! Where on earth did you get it?'

'At the market. Johnny bought it for me, in case I got sunstroke. Isn't it super! We bought one for you as well.'

'In case I got sunstroke waiting for you?'

'Did you? I'm sorry.'

'No, I'm teasing, pet. Go on.'

'We got some material for curtains – I'll get it.' Venetia went into the hall and brought in her shopping bounty, unrolling the material for Della's appraisal. 'What do you think?'

Della stood back, pretending to shade her eyes. 'It'll brighten the place up. And it'll match, certainly. Everything. Name the colour and it's there.' She pounced. 'Is this my hat?'

'Mm. It looks charming with that bathrobe. Oh, I do like it here.' Venetia collapsed full length on Della's bed and clasped her hands under her head, her eyes gazing dreamily ceilingward.

Della removed the sun-hat, which actually looked most attractive on her, and surveyed her friend for a moment or so, her piquant features expressive. Then she nodded. 'So that's how it is! Quick work for a little greenhorn in the male stakes.'

'I'll be working for him. He's the agricultural expert.'

Venetia closed her eyes and sighed blissfully. 'He has three reports he wants me to type out.'

'What bliss!'

'Isn't it? Della, I think I'm in love.'

'You don't say! Do you think you could in-love yourself off my bed and take your shopping orgy somewhere else? I want to get changed.'

'Certainly. I don't expect you to understand.' Venetia stood up, gathered up the material and wound it round herself, draping one end over her head and letting it flow behind, and stuck her hat on top at a rakish angle. Her tip-tilted nose tilted a little more, she drifted airily towards the door. 'I feel sorry for you. You can't have any notion of what it's like up here on this exalted plane of love.

'No?' Della chuckled, and slung the basket after her. 'But I know what it's like when somebody sticks a pin in cloud nine and it collapses. Try to get off first, sweetie. Just in case Johnny doesn't happen to be around to catch the pieces.'

'I'm shattered already. You're just jealous.'

But there was only another chuckle following her through the closing door.

*　　　*　　　*

An enormous African moon was bathing the night in silver when the two girls set off to stroll the short distance to Jason's bungalow. They were both rather silent, except for the melody Della hummed absently in soft, intermittent snatches, and Venetia's thoughts were too happily engaged in daydreams she did not want to divulge, even to the friendly, teasing Della.

All the lights were on the Kinlay bungalow, and another figure approached from the opposite direction as the girls entered the white gate. It was a woman, of medium height and solid muscular build. She wore a plain tailored two-piece of saxe blue linen and her grey hair was cut in a crop of uncompromising severity. Under the big lantern on the veranda she stopped and said without preamble: 'You must be the new girls. Welcome to Lake Karimba. I'm Muriel Vanders.'

'How do you do,' said Venetia formally, feeling as though she had suddenly been transported back to school-days and the first day of term under a new headmistress. But Della was not so affected. She disengaged her hand from Doctor Vanders' somewhat masculine grip and said gaily: 'How's the bug business here?'

'Slack. This crowd's disgustingly healthy – mind you two stay the same way. Shall we go in? Nobody stands on ceremony here.' Dr. Vanders led the way in and added an aside: 'My voice carries better than any doorbell.'

She did have a deep, penetrating voice and it brought a scurry of light, tip-tapping steps from the room on the left. A slender blonde emerged, sparkling in pale, silvery green lurex. She saw Della, stopped, and flung out both hands.

'Della! Darling! So you got here at last. And this is Venetia.' Her quick effusive smile flashed and surprisingly cold fingers brushed limply against Venetia's.

Close to, Claire's slender, apparent youthfulness was betrayed. There were fine lines about her eyes, and a certain febrile restlessness threatened to define itself be-tween the high arched brows and round the small, slightly pouting mouth. She also wore rather too much make-up. But her smile seemed friendly enough as she asked, 'And how do you like Kalawi? It's your first time out, isn't it?'

Venetia started to reply, but Claire had already turned back to Della, while calling over her shoulder: 'Jason, drinks, darling. A cosy one before the men arrive. I'm so sorry I wasn't here when you got here yesterday, but I stayed rather late at the Andrews' in Mortonstown and decided to stay overnight – I'm terrified of night driving.'

Della murmured a response, and the quick brittle tones went on: 'But I knew Jason would meet you and everything. He's longing to talk business again with someone who understands his ropes.'

Jason put a drink in Venetia's hand and there was a flicker of compression at the corners of his mouth, although his eyes held kindness for her as he enquired if she'd settled in comfortably at the bungalow. For a few moments he exchanged courteous pleasantries until Claire's high imperial, 'Darling!' took him away with a murmured apology.

Venetia sat down and caught Dr. Vanders' dry glance. She smiled shyly and the older woman returned it, her rather stern features softening with warmth. 'I expect you're feeling a little strange,' she said.

'Yes,' Venetia admitted, 'it's all strange but very wonderful to me. This is my first time abroad.'

'This is my first time too – at least for Africa,' Dr. Vanders said. 'I did three years in Karachi and another two in Mexico, then a spell with W.H.O. Actually I'm filling in here for a couple of months while Tubby Miles has a much needed leave. I think they'll be glad when he's back,' she added ruefully. 'They're not awfully happy about a woman medic on a project like this, but I was coming here in any case, so it fitted in conveniently.'

'What will you be doing when Dr. Miles comes back?' Venetia asked.

'Establishing the new ante-natal care and maternity training unit in the new resettlement area. A job considered much more suitable for me.' She smiled wryly and looked up as deep voices sounded outside. 'Here are the boys. I shall be teasing them about suddenly sprucing up for the new personnel.'

Claire's voice quickened and her whole being became animated with the restless brittle gestures which Venetia soon recognized as characteristic of the older girl's nervous, volatile temperament. Claire seemed to switch on and off like a light, Venetia thought, watching her greet the three men, toss the imperative order, 'Drinks, darling,' to Jason, and then flop on the couch with sinuous grace and sigh at the heat, apparently oblivious of the exchange of glances between Jason and Della as Jason turned to mix the drinks. Jason's glance held a trace of well disciplined resignation and Della's a warm understanding. Then the moment was gone in the handing out of glasses and forgotten in the warm smile Johnny sent winging across the room to Venetia.

But he did not come to her side, merely returned her softly whispered 'Hi' and remained to talk to Della and Jason beside the black glass table on which the drinks were spread.

Simon Manville, informal but still immaculate in beige dacron pants and a crisp, coffee-coloured shirt, moved towards Claire and bent to hear something she obviously intended only for his ears. He smiled, tendered her a cigarette and lit it for her, and the other man came towards Dr. Vanders.

'This is Drew Chalmers – our chief construction engineer.' Dr. Vanders completed the introduction and the newcomer took Venetia's hand in a grip that made her wince. He was a big man, about Jason's contemporary in age, Venetia decided, liking him instinctively, but for all his broad muscular strength he was quietly spoken and did not seem inclined either to parties or small talk. He dropped into the chair next to Venetia and presently out came the snapshots of his wife and two children.

42

'I'm expecting to hear any day that she's on her way here,' he said, tucking the pictures carefully back in his pocketbook. 'She has a young sister living in Kampala whom she hasn't seen for eight years, and three-year-old twin nephews, so she decided to make a special holiday occasion this year and come out to see them, then spend a few days here before she goes home.'

'And have a second honeymoon?' queried Dr. Vanders, smiling.

'If the dam doesn't decide to collapse that week.' He stood up and took the empty glasses from the doctor and Venetia as Claire started to marshal her guests into the dining-room.

To her disappointment Venetia found herself seated between Drew and Simon at the opposite end of the table to where Johnny was placed between Della and Claire. In the way that it happens sometimes at formally seated meals Venetia found Drew's head was turned more often to Dr. Vanders on his other side and Simon Manville's toward Della, who was his other table neighbour.

But it was an admirable meal; spiced chicken with groundnut sauce and little golden fried balls of savoury herbs and a palm leaf salad, and an exotic array of luscious unfamiliar fruits. Venetia tried to quell her disappointment; after all, she'd had a gorgeous afternoon. All the same, it didn't look as though she was going to have much chance to talk to him tonight . . .

'You're very quiet.'

She turned to meet Simon Manville's dark regard.

'Oh, I'm not naturally noisy – thank you.' She accepted sugar from the little silver bowl he offered.

Under cover of the clink of coffee spoons he asked softly: 'What happened to you today?'

'Nothing. I went shopping.' She glanced at him appre-

43

hensively from under the veil of her lashes, uncertain whether he was being mockingly indulgent or inquisitional. 'Is there any law against going shopping?'

'No.' He stirred his coffee. 'Only against the time you took.'

Venetia's shoulders stiffened and she turned indignantly. 'We were given the day off. Why shouldn't we take the chance to look round? Anyway, Mr. Kinlay said so,' she added defensively.

'Yes – to find your bearings round the site and settle in, not take a fifty-mile joyride.' He ignored her gasp of astonishment at this unwarranted censure and went on: 'Your friend took the opportunity to make a preliminary acquaintance with routine here and find out which jobs most required her attention.'

Now she knew he was absolutely serious, as objectionably arrogant as he had been last night. She remembered something and set down her cup sharply. 'So did I. I also arranged my routine, and discussed business with Mr. Slade, for whom I shall be working. To start with I have three reports to type for him and I shall be making that my first job tomorrow morning – at eight o'clock.'

'No, you won't,' he said with cool deliberation, 'at eight o'clock tomorrow morning you'll report to me.'

'You.'

'You heard.' A muscle twitched in the lean jaw. 'I'm sorry to upset the mistaken inference you appear to have formed, but you won't be working for friend Johnny, you'll be working for me.'

Dismay chilled her as the full implication of his statement sank in and she stared at him. At last she managed, 'But what about Johnny's reports? Somebody'll have to do them. There isn't anybody else. I thought that was why I got the job, because I understand the—'

'Don't fret, you'll have time to fit them in as well. But I also have a couple of reports waiting, plus a trayful of letters that are getting so flyblown they're almost obliterated. So I'll expect you promptly – I want to be up at the construction site by nine and I don't want to have to hang around waiting to explain things to you. If you'd spared half an hour this afternoon it would have been a help.'

Venetia struggled for a suitable response and a light voice spoke behind, reproachfully.

'Oh, Simon! Don't bully the child – you are a brute.' Claire leaned over between the two chairs and smiled winningly into his face. 'She only got here last night, have a heart. Don't let him bully you, poppet.' Claire turned her shining golden head and smiled sympathetically. 'Things have gone a bit haywire this week and he's worried. Now come and have a drink – this is supposed to be a party, not a briefing session, so you can forget work for once, Simon, even if Jason can't.' Still pretending to chide, she playfully took their hands in hers as though they were children and steered them through to the lounge. There she made an attractive grimace at Simon and said sternly: 'I can see I'll have to mix you one of my specials – you need thawing out.'

This last observation voiced Venetia's sentiments so exactly that she could have laughed, if she hadn't felt so furious – and hurt. If only she dared make such a remark outright to him!

And he was going to be her boss!

CHAPTER THREE

FORTUNATELY, however, for Venetia's secret apprehension she did not have the intimidating Mr. Manville breathing authority down her neck all day. After that first briefing in the plain, barely furnished office, sitting under the drone of the cooling fan over the table at which she would work, she did not see a great deal of her new boss. But she did have quite a number of other visitors.

It was surprising how many of the men, the engineers, the electrical experts, the foremen, the aides and the keymen, found it necessary to come down to base during that first week on one pretext or another and pop into Venetia's – or rather the senior settlement officer's! – office to see the new feminine addition, and that first week Venetia and Della found themselves on the receiving end of more coffees and drinks in the little building known as the rec than they could possibly drink. As Della said, it seemed a pity they were all in camp up at the main site of the construction – a regret, however, which Venetia did not share. They were mostly a tough, hard-drinking and impudent crowd and she was not sorry when the visits tailed off, nor to hear from Della that Jason had not missed the comings and goings and had acted accordingly.

'We're going to be horribly protected,' sighed Della, 'and the construction site is out of bounds to *us*, just in case we get any ideas – not that I'd want to go up there among all the mess and concrete dust.' She laughed. 'Jason's having a swap round. I'm being moved into his own sanctum and Mac is shifting accounts into the outer office so that nobody has an excuse to wander through any more.'

'It's the same over the road,' Venetia said. 'Simon Manville practically threw out two of the construction engineers this morning – they wanted me to go on a jaunt to Mortonstown tonight.'

'Spoilsport! How are you getting along with him?'

'So-so,' Venetia sighed. 'I suppose he thinks he's protecting me, actually I've never met such a tough crowd – do you know what one of them suggested?'

'The worst?' grinned Della.

'No, that they draw lots to take us out. Sauce!' She sighed. 'I suppose I should be grateful that Simon Manville isn't like that, but he does make me feel like an innocent that couldn't look after herself. It's not working out a bit like we thought it would, is it?' she added with another sigh.

'Meaning Johnny?'

'I hardly ever see him,' said Venetia sadly. 'He just pops in, hands me the work he wants done, and pops out again.'

'It'll settle down, pet,' Della said sympathetically, 'it's early days, and this evening social whirl will die off as well.'

Venetia wandered across to the window and stared at the sunset over the lake. 'What are we going to wear for our housewarming? I wish I'd known more of what it's like here, I'd have brought more clothes – more dressy gear. I thought it would be more remote, more like army life. Whatever army life is like. I didn't know they'd be entertaining every night.'

'They didn't till we came,' said Della. 'Our arrival combined with Claire coming out and Dr. Vanders being locum is the cause. Suddenly there are four women around the place and Claire is a socialite at any time, so it's an

47

excuse for her to try to liven things up a bit. All the same . . .' Della looked thoughtfully at the crisp lime green dress and jacket which Tobi, the houseboy, had just brought back from laundering. 'I know what you mean, Ven. When I think of Claire's get-up last night!'

'Think of it at any time. She changes about six times a day. Every time I see her she has something different on.'

Della's mouth turned down slightly at the corners. 'Of course one does have to change more often to stay fresh, but Jason says she brought a department store of clothes with her. Oh well, I mustn't be bitchy, I suppose. Come on, time we stirred ourselves.'

Certainly a burst of entertaining had hit the base with the advent of the girls. In succession the crowd dined with Dr. Vanders, Drew Chalmers, Johnny, when Claire took it on herself to act as his hostess, and then again with the Kinlays, by which time the girls had somewhat hurriedly organized the stark little prefabricated building into a semblance of a bungalow home. Venetia spent most of the week-end sewing the new curtains which added a colourful note of gaiety and then they were ready to return hospitality with a housewarming which was voted greatly successful even if exhausting.

Then suddenly everything seemed to go flat.

Labour trouble developed again up at the construction site and a consignment of new equipment including certain vital components failed to arrive on the scheduled delivery date. Drew Chalmers' language seared the telegraph wires and Jason's brow seemed permanently furrowed. Simon Manville was due to go to Mortonstown to attend a three-day high level conference with the Kawali Development Council, and Claire suddenly decided she'd heard enough of dam troubles and another taste of civilization with her friends in the capital was indicated. She departed with Simon and the girls found themselves with time on their hands.

'Not that I'm sorry,' said Della one evening a few days later, pouring her sundowner and stretching herself out on the lounger. 'Are you still writing letters, girl?'

'This is the last one,' Venetia did not look up, 'then I shouldn't have to write any more for at least six weeks, by the time these get there, and they all write back,' she added hopefully if somewhat incoherently. 'Haven't you done yours?'

'I never write letters if I can help it. I sent those picture postcards off from the airport, they'll do for the time being. What *is* more important is a full beauty session. I could do with one – and so could you, my pet. We mustn't let our skins dry out.'

'We haven't been here long enough – how do you spell parallel?'

'What an odd word to crop up! Put in three ells and be on the safe side. I wish I'd brought some colour wash shampoo, I'm sure the sun is bringing some reddish glints in my hair.'

Della was particularly fussy about her rich, blue-black tresses and Venetia glanced up briefly. 'It isn't.'

'Wonder if there's a decent hairdresser in Mortonstown.'

'Claire will know.'

'I'll know soon myself – we'll be due for a long weekend at the end of the month.' Della studied her neat beige sandals thoughtfully. 'I think I'll buy a new outfit. I fancy all white.'

Venetia nodded, forgetting her letter. 'I fancy one of those pyjama suits with the deep plunge at the back – I wonder what my copper medallion would look like if I wore it down the back.'

Della grinned, 'First lesson, sweetie, try to be original. I must admit that rose silk set looked trendy on Claire, but I can't see you in them – like an English wild rose disguised as Mata Hari. Oh, bother! Who's this?'

'It's Johnny.'

He came from the verandah and Venetia's heart did its now customary caper at the sight of him. Della waved lazily at the remains of the drinks left over after the party and he went to help himself. 'Heard the news?' he enquired.

'No. Don't tell me last month's papers have arrived.'

'No, we're going to have our own movies.'

'In the moonlight? I can't wait!'

'Simon is going to bring the projector and screen back from town.'

'And the movies? Vintage?'

'Well, it'll be a change. Will you sit in the back row with me?'

'No can,' Della laughed at him. 'I'm short-sighted. Whoever thought of that one?'

'It'll be a change.' Johnny glanced at the writing pad on Venetia's knee and back to Della. 'You haven't been here long enough to get bored. Wait till you've been here a couple of years.'

'Pessimist!' Della gave him an innocent look. 'I was under the impression that the dam was scheduled for opening – or is it launching? – in November.'

'The way things are going it'll be next November, so prepare yourself. Still, there are compensations.' His glance held meaning and Venetia suppressed a sigh, not wanting to admit her interpretation of that meaning, even though it had become more obvious every time Johnny was near Della. A step sounded and a shadow fell across the verandah. Venetia turned. 'Here's Jason.'

There was a small exclamation from Johnny, but Della was suddenly alert, her careless banter fading. She said, 'You'll have to excuse me, kids. Jason has to be at the site all day tomorrow and we've some paperwork to get through.' She stood up and put her glass back on the tray, subtly sloughing off her air of indolence. 'Johnny, are you killing time?'

'More or less.'

'Would you pick up a couple of dozen cokes and lemons for us? We're practically out. I meant to send Tobi down before he went off, but I forgot.'

'It'll be a pleasure, but you know you have to send a signed chit if you send the houseboy for anything from the store? And that includes me!'

'Heavens, yes.' Della waved to Jason to come in from where he stood just outside the screens, his brows quirked upwards. 'Ven, be a pet and go down and sign for them. I think we'd better get in a stock of lager for the male guests who drop in.'

'Africa's quite a thirst-raiser,' remarked Jason, strolling in and depositing a bulging folder on the side table. He nodded to Johnny and gave Venetia an apologetic glance. 'Am I going to be in the way here?'

'No, of course not,' she said hastily, still a little in awe of Jason in spite of his friendliness. 'I was going out for a meander anyway.'

Johnny seemed more silent than usual during the walk down to the rec, and Venetia wondered unhappily if he had realized that Della had quite blatantly contrived the errand on which they were now bound. The lemonade and the cans of beer could have waited until tomorrow ... But Johnny's smile was as good-humoured as ever when they found the rec deserted and the little adjoining storeroom locked. They went in search of Mac, the duty store officer, and got the key from him, and when Venetia had selected an assortment of mineral waters and a dozen cans of beer Johnny stacked them neatly in a small crate. He put the crate on a table in the rec, locked up the storeroom, then said: 'Come on, I'll play you for half-pennies.'

'Play what?'

'Darts.' From a ledge under an ancient, well pitted dartboard he picked up the flight and held them out to her. 'Ladies first.'

'But I can't play darts!' She began to laugh. 'I couldn't hit the wall, let alone that board.'

'That means I'll win – good! You don't want to go straight back, do you? I don't think Della's going to be sociable tonight.'

There was a record player in one corner of the hut and a pile of well-worn seven-inch forty-fives. Johnny switched the machine on and put on the top record from the pile, then came back to her side. Somewhat warily she stood where he indicated. After her first two shots had gone as far wide as she had expected she managed by a beginner's fluke to score a treble with her third and earned Johnny's exuberant congratulations. Some time later she was richer by three pence and he said suddenly, 'Let's have a drink.'

'What do you do here in your spare time?' she asked when they had replenished the record supply and got their drinks.

He shrugged. 'Play cards, darts, stay in our own places and read. Most of us go into Mortonstown for our long weekends, but it's a rough trip to do in one evening. The track is a shocker for about thirty miles after you leave Noyali. I broke a spring the first time I tried it, so unless anybody gets bush blues too badly we don't bother between times. Last year we tried to organize this place ourselves. Somebody contributed the record player and Steve – he's gone now – bequeathed us the dartboard, and it's taken for granted that all reading matter ends up down here in the common pool.' He glanced round the whitewashed walls, bare of colour except a few fading pin-ups of the cutie variety, and gave an exclamation of derision. 'Through your eyes it must look a poor joint. Somehow we've never been able to capture the atmosphere of ye olde English pub.'

He got out his cigarettes and she was silent, thinking of the long evenings of the two years here without recreation and the amenities people at home took for granted. She was about to speak when Johnny said lightly: 'And how are you two going to amuse yourselves while you're here?'

'We'll think of something.'

He grinned. 'You'd better. You haven't had time to get bored yet, but you will.'

'I can't imagine it. Everything's so different and fascinating.' She drew up the last drop of coke through her straw and asked idly, 'What's Mortonstown like?'

'Okay. Nice little town, a smaller edition of Nairobi but not so well laid out. The main shopping centre is along the Parade, and there's a big market.' He paused, 'I'll be going through next weekend, so if there's anything you want bringing back just let me know – provided it isn't personal feminine fripperies,' he added warningly.

'I think they could wait until I go myself,' she said, 'but thanks all the same.'

'When you do, don't be tempted to stay at the Golden Falls – it'll break you. An American friend of mine said it was an extra dollar on the bill every time the waiter

53

snapped his fingers – she said they sure did a lot of finger-snapping.'

She nodded, and he added, 'Stay at the New Africa, it's just as comfortable and more reasonable, unless, of course, you want to be fashionable.'

'I don't. I find fashionable hotels terrifying.'

She lapsed into silence, wondering who was the American 'she' who had sampled the luxury of Kawali's premier tourist hotel, and the gap lengthened while Johnny drained the last of his lager and looked idly at the lettering on the can. The record stopped and she got up to turn it to its reverse side. Over the opening strains of *Some Enchanted Evening* she heard the door of a vehicle slam with metallic hollowness and as she turned round the rec door swung open and Simon Manville walked in.

There was dust on the knees of his fawn slacks and traces of oil on his sunburnt hands. 'That lousy track – I had a burst. Sling me a cooler, Johnny,' he said without preamble. His glance ranged over Venetia and betrayed a flicker of surprise at seeing her there. It was only momentary, however, and he eyed the empties on the table. 'Not teaching our new secretary bad habits, I hope.'

Johnny grinned, looking highly delighted at his friend's return, and shook his head. 'Not guilty. She's strictly on the coke wagon – don't you trust me?'

'No.' Simon sat down and took a long swig at the can Johnny had opened. Over the rim he regarded her dispassionately. 'And I don't trust this young innocent to realize the effects of too much alcohol in this climate. There's been a bit too much bottle-hitting since they arrived.'

Venetia's earlier mood of relaxation had faded, to be replaced by a wariness which was becoming second nature when Simon Manville was around. Suddenly she felt annoyance at his interruption. 'Not by me,' she said coldly, 'I'm a rotten shot. I couldn't hit a bottle any better than that dartboard behind you. And not so much of the young innocent!' she added furiously, aware of Johnny's amusement, 'unless you want me to start calling you Dad!'

Unexpectedly he began to laugh. 'But you are young, little one, and what would you say if I said you weren't innocent?' His eyes teased and openly challenged, then he reached forward and rubbed her cheek with a rough yet tender gesture. 'All right, you're not – and I've left a smudge on your face to add to the blight on your evening.' His smile ebbed and he turned to Johnny. 'Anything happened?'

Johnny shrugged. 'I had Chief M'goli to see me yesterday. The Noyali waterhole's getting low. You can guess the rest.'

'Yes. Blame the dam. So much for Jason's hopes that it would last out till the rains got going. Did you inspect?'

Johnny nodded. 'A week at the most. I think we're going to have to put in that temporary pipeline. How went things at your end?'

'We finalized the Oskiri boundary line, thank God. Apart from that, little else.' Simon sighed and there were traces of weariness round his eyes. He stood up. 'I'll run you back. I've a load of Claire's gear to drop off at the Kinlay place.'

'She didn't come back with you?' asked Venetia, feeling it was time she contributed something to the conversation.

'No, she's coming back on the Tuesday plane, with Mrs. Chalmers and young Mallard's fiancée.'

'Which means more celebrations – cheers!' Johnny slung the crate of drinks into the back of Simon's tourer and winked at Venetia. 'You'd better get your bottle-aiming eye into focus.'

'She's going to obey the rules. Come on, pint-size, in you get.'

Sighing, Venetia obeyed, sitting small and silent between the two men as Simon put the tourer into motion. It skimmed round the turning circle with a fine disregard for centrifugal force and Johnny put a steadying arm round her shoulders as Simon sent the vehicle haring up the strip road. Her resentment of him was born anew. Did he have to drive so fast? They'd be there in thirty seconds! It would have been infinitely preferable to walk back with Johnny, through the soft dusky night under the bright frosting of the Southern Cross.

Nursing her disappointment and breathlessly aware of Johnny's firm warm closeness against her, poor Venetia forgot about the crate he would have been carrying . . .

More as a formality than anything else she asked the men if they were coming in for a drink and did not press the invitation when Simon refused rather brusquely for both of them. He remained at the wheel while Johnny carried in the crate, bowed gallantly to Della who had come out on to the verandah and murmured something to her in a way that seemed almost secretive to the watching Venetia before departing with a final good night salute.

The sound of the vehicle faded and Della raised enquiring brows. 'Well? . . .'

'Anything but.' Venetia's mouth drooped. 'We played darts and the band played *Some Enchanted Evening*, but Johnny's turned tone deaf as far as I'm concerned and Simon Manville arrived.'

'Oh dear . . .' Della walked into the brightness of the lounge and closed the screens. 'I'm sorry, pet.'

'It's not your fault,' said Venetia despondently. 'It's just that . . . on that first day when he bought me the sun-hat he said he was going to arrange things, a picnic or something, and that was as far as it got. Oh, well . . .' she sighed, and for the first time noticed a certain air of élan about her friend. 'You're looking very bright-eyed about something,' she observed.

'Me?' Della shook her head and assumed an innocent expression. 'I'm always bright-eyed. But, darling, are you sure . . .? Have you had a look at your own face?'

'What?' Venetia instinctively put her hand up to her face. Then she remembered and let her hand drop. 'It's nothing, just . . .' She trailed out and made for the mirror in her bedroom.

In their passing Simon Manville's knuckles *had* deposited two small browny smudges of oil on the soft rose curve that was just beginning to betray the first deepening tint of golden sundust.

For a moment she stood motionless, wondering if it would have made any difference if he had not come to make three out of two, and for the first time she admitted the suspicion which had begun that first evening at Jason's. Johnny's interest was turning towards Della, and even though Della was playing fair and making no effort at all to encourage his interest – or anyone else's – it wasn't going to make any difference.

Venetia sighed and reached for tissues and cleansing cream. The lighthearted little wager in which she and Della had indulged wasn't working out at all according to plan. So much for the only bet she had ever won in her life. Her triumphant flip of a coin was going to lose after all. . .

*   *   *

As Johnny had forecast, the advent of Drew Chalmers' wife and the tall attractive fiancée of Keith Mallard provided the excuse for another spate of celebrations. The visitors were to stay for several days, and even though Venetia formed the impression that Jean Chalmers would have preferred to spend as much of the time Drew had free quietly with him-Claire could not resist exerting her organizing capabilities.

The day after their arrival was earmarked for a drive to the market where Johnny had taken Venetia on that first day. But this time she found herself in the back of the runabout with Keith and the gay, self-possessed Kirstie while Della rode in front beside Johnny. It was a very hot, dry afternoon without a trace of breeze to relieve the oppressiveness, and the stalls were as varied and colourful and fascinating as before, but the magic had gone for Venetia. The gay straw basket she had brought with her remained empty and on the return journey she found herself in Simon Manville's tourer.

'Cheer up,' he said after the first ten minutes of silence.

'I'm fine,' she said lamely, looking away from the vehicle ahead from which floated the laughter of Claire and Kirstie and Della.

'That,' he said in a low voice, 'is the only thing about you that isn't obvious.' He dropped back a little, allowing the distance to increase between the tourer and the vehicle in front to avoid the throwback of dust.

She stared at the passing scene. 'And what is that supposed to mean?'

'Among other things that you don't appear to have enjoyed the return visit to Nykuni.'

Her glance slid towards him and away again. Why should it matter to Simon Manville whether she had enjoyed herself or not? And why was he bothering to indulge in this verbal digging? He – he couldn't have guessed! Surely that wasn't what he meant, that she was being obvious about Johnny. A panicky thought came; did men talk about girls the same way as girls talked about men? These two seemed to be pretty close friends . . . She took a deep breath and said coolly:

'You had plenty to say the last time. The time when I apparently enjoyed myself *too* much.'

'Did I?' An undertone of amusement ran through his voice. 'But I've done nothing to put a blight on your enjoyment today, have I?'

She resisted the temptation of a childish affirmative and after a few moments of silence he said lightly: 'Perhaps it isn't one of your days for shining.'

'I don't shine to order,' she said flatly, 'and I've no intention of trying.'

He did not reply, his attention concentrated on a particularly treacherous section of the track, and just as she had decided that he was going to leave her to brood in peace he said dryly: 'I can see that, but there are occasions when it pays to try.'

The infuriating saneness of this advice did nothing to inspire an instant desire to act on it, and she had never felt less like shining when the vehicle rolled back into base, just in time to see Johnny lift Della down from the runabout, swing her round gaily, and keep her close within the curve of his arm while they stood talking to Jason, who had emerged from Admin to enquire how everyone had enjoyed the jaunt.

The sight of that strong arm, the glint of its sprinkling of sun-bleached hairs and deep tan accentuated against the cool green slimness of Della's waist invoked a painful conflict of dejection and scorn for her own hurt jealousy in Venetia. Suddenly she wished she and Della had never made that silly little wager; it wouldn't have given her the idea that all she had to do was smile on Johnny and wait for fate – and Johnny – to smile back. Somehow it would have made it easier to accept the painful fact that Johnny might have ideas of his own . . .

She shook her head uncertainly and walked slowly towards the bungalow. It was stupid to be jealous or resentful of Della, who couldn't help being so undeniably attractive and who, in spite of her confidence and abilities, hadn't a scrap of meanness or bitchiness in her nature. She would just have to make up her mind to accept it, she certainly wasn't going to run after Johnny, or let Della guess how much it hurt. But it wasn't going to be easy to stand back and . . . This afternoon had been . . . She thought of the tentatively arranged outing for the following day.

Claire had suggested a trip to Lizard Rocks, a place in the hills at the far side of the lake, where a series of miniature falls tumbled down to a pool which was safe for swimming. There was also a baboon colony nearby and a particular species of beautifully marked lizards to be seen. The plan was for a leisurely morning drive, a swim, a barbecue lunch and a laze round before returning to Claire's for the evening.

It sounded inviting enough, and at any other time Venetia would have looked forward to it with impatience and zest, but now . . . suddenly she felt as though she didn't care whether she went or not. She knew Dr. Vanders had cried off, pleading work, and Jason of course could not go, and Kirstie had privately remarked that she would have preferred to spend the day on her own with her fiancé, but out of politeness she would probably fall in with Claire's arrangements. Venetia sighed; she supposed she would have to do the same . . .

Preoccupied with her thoughts, she did not notice that

Della was unusually thoughtful that evening, until just as Venetia was about to take a shower before going to bed Della called suddenly: 'Ven!'

Venetia stopped at the door, her robe over her arm, then slowly went into Della's room. The older girl was sitting at the shelf unit which served as dressing table and her mirrored face showed a shadow of concern. Without turning, she said slowly: 'I'd better tell you now that Johnny has asked me to spend next weekend with him at Mortonstown.'

There was a small exclamation and an echoed, 'Weekend!' and Della, mistaking the inflection, swung round, a faint smile coming to her mouth. 'Not that kind of a weekend, pet. There's no need to sound so scandalized.'

'No, I didn't mean that. I—' Venetia sat on the edge of the bed and tried to smile. 'I just—'

'Got a surprise? I was afraid of that.' Della reached for her cigarettes and after lighting one tossed them and the lighter on the bed. 'I didn't angle for the invitation, you know that, don't you?'

'Yes, of course. Are – are you going?'

'I'd like to.'

'Then why not?' Venetia kept her tone unconcerned and got up to get an ashtray. 'Go and enjoy yourself.'

Della bit her lip and looked worriedly at the small set features. At last she said, 'I'm sorry, pet, I did try to keep off the grass, honestly.'

'I know you did, and I don't blame you. It just happened that way.'

'Yes ...' Della reached for her moisture cream and began stroking it into her slender throat. 'You know, I can't help thinking that it might turn out for the best in the long run. I don't think you're cut out for casual affairs, pet. I'm very much afraid that when the inevitable ending came you'd be hurt. Better a little hurt now before it goes too deep than heartbreak later on when you'd got too fond of him.'

Venetia was silent, knowing in her heart that Della was invariably wise and usually right, and in this case unerringly so. She said, 'What about you?'

'Johnny and I speak the same language and we understand each other. He won't get hurt any more than I will. But there's something else . . .' Della's hands ceased their methodical plying of cream and the dark hint of concern was back in her eyes. 'I would like to accept this invitation, and the inevitable pairing-off it's bound to lead to, because I'm beginning to see some way ahead and I . . .' Della stopped and looked down at her hands, for once seeming uncertain of herself.

A trace of puzzlement flitted over Venetia's face and she said hastily, 'For heaven's sake don't worry about me. It – it was a daft idea in the first place, anyway.'

'Wasn't it?' Della's smile was mirthless. 'I'm afraid I can't see myself hitting it off with Simon Manville.'

'Which only leaves Johnny.' Venetia stubbed out her half smoked cigarette and stood up. 'I understand. I don't ring any bells for him, so one of us might as well enjoy his company.' At the door she stopped and forced a smile. 'Who knows? It might turn out to be the real thing this time.'

'I doubt it.'

It did not occur to Venetia until some time later that there had been a strange expression of relief on Della's lovely features as she added: 'Your turn will come, pet, and when it does you won't even be giving the Johnnies of this world a second glance, let alone a wasted heartache.'

CHAPTER FOUR

By the following morning Venetia had sadly decided against joining the outing to Lizard Rocks. She just wasn't yet adjusted to seeing Della 'paired off' with Johnny.

With her usual sympathy of perception Della did not attempt to persuade her to change her mind, and when Venetia said that she was supposed to be working anyway and the backlog would only pile up Della exclaimed wryly, 'Don't make my guilt complex any worse, for goodness' sake,' then added hopefully, 'but you might stand by in case Jason wants anything while I'm missing.'

Venetia gave an assurance to this effect and had settled down at the typewriter, not without a certain sense of smug rectitude, well before the pleasure-seekers set off.

When the cars had gone the base seemed quiet. Mac and his African assistant disappeared into the store office and from where Venetia sat she could see the two Bantu boys tending the brilliant scarlet flower beds in front of the Admin. office at the other side of the road. The Citroen was standing in its customary place under the side awning and on a sudden impulse Venetia picked up the house phone and pressed the buzzer for Jason's sanctum.

A deep voice that didn't sound like Jason's said 'Yes?' rather abruptly, and then, as she blinked, added, 'Manville here.'

'Oh . . .' Stumbling a little, she said, 'I – I – it's Venetia here. I wondered if Mr. Kinlay wanted any let—'

'Venetia!' The voice held a tinge of surprise, wasn't quite so impersonal. 'Why aren't you with the others? They've gone, you know. A good ten minutes ago.'

'I know.' She smiled faintly. Trust Simon Manville to assume instantly that she'd managed to miss the take-off! 'I didn't particularly want to go and there is a lot of work waiting.'

'Yes,' he said dryly, 'it's time somebody got down to work again round here. I—' He broke off and there was a faint interchange in the background, then he said, 'Here's Jason now.'

Jason also sounded a trifle surprised and amused, but a few minutes later, on his instruction, she was sitting at Della's desk over in Admin. and Jason, with solemn indulgence, was dictating the day's letters. Somehow, after that, the day didn't seem so bad. Air-conditioning kept the enervating heat at bay and at ten-thirty she had coffee and biscuits with Jason and Simon, and at noon was invited to have a leisurely lunch with them.

For once Simon Manville refrained from the sardonic little digs he seemed to reserve for her, but how much this disarming approach stemmed from Jason's presence she had no means of knowing. If only all bosses were like Jason, she reflected. He was warm, friendly and courteous, yet he had an underlying strength and decisiveness that bespoke natural authority and commanded instant respect. She suspected that anyone who underestimated him would be in for an unpleasant shock. It was just that he knew how to get the best out of people and when to relax the reins. No wonder Della adored working for him. But perhaps she had misjudged Simon Manville, she decided at four o'clock after Jason bade her to pack up for the day, and her own boss said casually: 'I'll see you to-night. We'll be along to pick you up about seven.' Jason wasn't here now!

Too surprised to do anything but murmur assent, she put the cover on the typewriter and went back to the

64

bungalow in search of tea. But the hurt returned with Della and Johnny an hour later, and the knowledge that she couldn't escape the evening ahead. Somehow she would have to pretend that she didn't care, that Johnny, with his tall outdoor handsomeness and carefree charm, had made her aware for the first time in her life of the spell a man could weave so quickly and without effort . . .

'I'm definitely going to splurge in Mortonstown,' announced Della gaily when they were waiting for the men. 'I've worn this thing three times already since I came.'

Worn three times or not, the sleeveless mandarin sheath of glowing jewel blue looked superb on Della, and beside her Venetia felt colourless in a pastel pink so delicate it seemed almost white under the brilliant fluorescent fitting Claire had had installed in her lounge.

Looking round the room, Venetia had to admit that Claire had accomplished wonders in the stark plainness of a prefabricated unit which had never been intended to be more than temporary living quarters supplied with only the minimum essentials needed by male personnel. Bright modern prints hung on the walls and small vivid cushions were scattered over the cane furniture, but a leopard skin stretched above a shelf of scarlet Swedish glassware struck a note more redolent of new town suburbia than the heart of Africa.

Keith Mallard was telling stories, and one of the senior engineers was itching to cap him. Kirstie was smiling to herself and wearing the expression of one who knew what was coming next, and Claire was quite wantonly appropriating Simon Manville's attention. A buffet table was loaded with the trappings which didn't seem to vary much between Kensington and Kawali, and Venetia suddenly wondered if this was what she had come to Africa for, to nibble tinned shrimps and little sausages on sticks, smoke and talk and drink and smile, and nibble shrimps and . . .

She saw Johnny approaching and turned away hastily. At the moment she couldn't bear to face him. She set down her drink and slipped behind Dr. Vanders and the Chalmers and let herself out through the screens.

The air was warm and fragrant with the scent of queen of the night, and she stood on the verandah, upturning her face to the velvety stillness. So many stars – she was sure there were more over Africa then anywhere else in the world – and so much dark sky made her feel small and lost and conscious of a sudden aching loneliness. She moved farther along the verandah until she was out of the spill of light from the screens and leaned on the rail, where in the anonymity of the darkness she could give way to her forlorn thoughts and a mixture of emotions that had never been so acute back home in England. She'd had dates, and she'd had a rave over a new boy in the department a couple of months ago, but looking back the boys she had known seemed immature compared to Johnny, and . . .

She did not hear the sound of approaching company until the rails gave slightly under her forearms and a scent of tobacco drifted to her nostrils. Simon Manville leaned on the rail beside her and said companionably:

'Communing with the stars again?'

'They're too far away,' she said sadly.

'And lacking in response?'

'I suppose so.'

A slight pause, then, 'Is this how you usually enjoy yourself at social gatherings?'

'Of course not! But it – it is hot, and – and—'

'Of course.' The rail gave slightly again. 'Like to tell

Uncle Simon about it?'

Uncle! She almost smiled. 'There isn't anything to tell.'

'There never is, but it's the little untold things that are saddest of all.' He dropped his cigarette end and ground it under his heel, then resumed his relaxed stance, this time turned slightly so that she could see his shadowed features outlined against the dark. 'It's Johnny, isn't it?' he stated.

'It isn't anybody,' she said wearily.

'And that's it – the first tentative jump that missed.'

She interlaced her fingers and stared down at them. 'There has to be a first time for everything.'

'You tried the wrong tactics, you know.'

Her head came up sharply. 'How do you know I tried any tactics? And anyway, even if I had, how do you know they were wrong?'

'Because Johnny won't get serious. I've been watching for the signs, and wondering how long it would be before you got hurt.'

'Well, now you know,' she said bitterly.

'I know this, little one, that a man likes to make the running. You might have made it with Johnny but for two things.'

'And so.' It was not a question, but he chose to ignore the flatness of her tone and continued thoughtfully:

'And so. First of all, you picked the wrong approach.'

'Really?' she said coldly. 'I wasn't aware of using any particular approach. I'm not in the habit of using artifice or pretending to be something which I'm not.'

'I can see that,' he commented dryly, 'all too clearly. You're so natural it's almost transparent.'

'Thank you!' She instilled as much sarcasm as she could into the words. 'Why don't you go the whole hog and say I'm colourless?'

67

'I meant nothing of the kind, and well you know it.'
A trace of exasperation crept into his tone. 'I'm merely
trying to tell you that Johnny likes his women sophisticated. He has no time for little girls.'

She digested this in silence for a few moments, then said
flatly, 'But I don't happen to be a little girl.'

'I didn't mean in the literal sense. You're at least
eighteen or Jason would never have allowed you out here.
You're also,' he paused to run a cool measuring glance
over the soft pale glow of her in the dimness, 'about five
foot two, and show all the rather obvious signs of certain
feminine distinctions that little girls don't have. But as
far as the man-woman correlation goes . . .' He shook his
head. 'You're still a baby.'

Venetia drew a deep breath and maintained temper and
coolness at somewhat difficult cost. So he thought she was
callow, did he? Well, she wasn't going to give him the
satisfaction of seeing he'd got her rattled. She lifted her
head proudly. 'Seeing that you're the self-styled expert,
perhaps you can suggest how I acquire twenty instant
years – without the wrinkles that go with them?'

A faint sound that could have been mirth escaped him,
but his voice sounded quite casual as he said, 'There are
ways and means – if they're worth it.'

'The artifices?'

'If you prefer to call them that.'

'I prefer honesty.'

'I know.' Imperceptibly his voice had softened. He
looked down at her. 'Listen, little one, I'm not trying to
needle you, or make fun of you. I know you're standing
there hating me, but hating me is preferable to going back
in there and watching what you don't want to see. You're
feeling pretty grim, aren't you? All hedged in so that you
can't get away, and another five months to have to stand

back while your best friend and Johnny have fun. And there doesn't seem to be a single thing you can do about it.'

'I'll just have to get over it, won't I?' she said tautly.

'And that's where the artifice comes in useful. But honesty doesn't have any. Are you going to let the world see?'

She remained stubbornly silent, wishing she were anywhere but here at this moment, yet strangely bound by some force she was reluctant to admit could only be emanating from the man at her side. At last she sighed. 'I suppose you're worried in case you're going to have a droopy face around your office. Well, you won't, I can assure you.'

'Do I appear worried at that grim prospect?'

Her mouth tightened. 'Then why are you bothered?'

He said softly, 'You're longing to have your first love affair, aren't you? And the spell of Africa has caught you pretty badly.'

'That's ridiculous!' she denied hotly, 'and you've no right to say such things.'

'Maybe. But I'm taking that right on myself,' he said coolly, and put a detaining hand over her wrist. 'No, don't run away yet. I haven't finished. Okay, so you want to fledge your wings. Well, there's nothing unusual about that – it would be abnormal if you didn't. So why not take a practice run first, and save your pride into the bargain?'

There was no need now for the restraining hand on her wrist. She stared at him, astonishment widening her eyes as she tried to fathom his expression through the shadows. 'A practice run? What do you mean? Are – are you trying to be funny? Because if you are I – I don't—'

'No. I'm trying to be helpful and practical. Let me

clarify further.' He took out his cigarettes and offered her one, lighting it and his own with calm, unhurried movements. 'It's quite simple. You've heard about fruit out of reach being sweetest? I am proposing to remove you out of Johnny's reach, whether he has second thoughts or not. Naturally you'll hope he does. But in the meantime you're going to have that practice run – with me.'

'W-with you?' She backed a pace. 'You mean . . .?'

'I mean we're going to have a flirtation. You and I. Don't pretend that that wasn't exactly what you and your friend had in mind. You didn't have any intentions of going in at the deep end. At least *you* didn't, I'm prepared to swear.'

'Yes, but . . .' She shook her head and bewilderment clouded her face. 'You must be crazy. We – we're not even – even—'

'Attracted?' His mouth curved sardonically. 'All the better. The experiment will be safer that way.'

'Yes, but . . .' She raised her hands and let them fall, still amazed by his startling proposition. An affair with Simon Manville. A practice run!

Suddenly he smiled. 'Now don't argue. Give it a fair trial. I rather fancy that when you see the results you'll have second thoughts about the craziness.' He took her arm and began to draw her along the verandah, speaking in rapid, lowered tones. 'You're going back in there with me, and you're going to stay at my side till it's over. Then you're going to leave with me. Understand?'

'The instructions are the only clear things, Mr. Manville.'

'Simon.'

'Yes – *Simon*! – and supposing I do. What then?'

'You'll have to wait and see, won't you?'

She stared up at the dark arrogant height of him as

he stood there, his hand on the latch of the screens and utter assurance that she would fall in with this preposterous idea radiating from every line of him, and an hysterical urge to laugh swept over her; it couldn't make sense! Not ... she became aware of the rise and fall of voices within the room and knew that the evening had reached the point where drink and informality begin to melt inhibitions, and the brief rush of inward mirth died abruptly. If she obeyed the dictate of her instincts she would about turn and make for the bungalow where sanity at least would prevail and she wouldn't have to wear a party face she didn't feel in the least like wearing. Then Simon's hand tightened on her arm and the suspicion came that a bolt for freedom wouldn't be easy just at the moment. Where Simon Manville was concerned it was a risk she hadn't the courage to take, the air about him portended purpose, and warning ...

A rush of warm, smoke-laden air met her as he drew open the screen and stood back for her to enter. The first thing she saw was Della standing at the far side of the room, her back to the wall, and beside her, very close, was Johnny.

He also leaned one shoulder negligently against the wall. He had a full glass in his hand, but he seemed to have forgotten it as he looked down into Della's face with the kind of expression Venetia had seen before on the faces of men who met Della. It was the kind of expression that enwrapped her and shut out everyone and everything else nearby.

Venetia swallowed hard. With a chill sense of loss she ceded to defeat and at the same moment a hard arm went firmly round her waist.

'Over there – a drink is indicated, I think. What would you like?'

71

'Anything, it doesn't matter,' she said tonelessly, allowing him to steer her over to the buffet table.

'Trusting little girl all of a sudden, aren't you?' he whispered in an ironic aside.

She shrugged, forcing herself to smile at Jason, who was chatting to Jean Chalmers and flashed her a friendly acknowledgment.

'A little of this, I think, and a jigger of that . . .' Simon was mixing and shaking, gravely intent on the task in hand. He frowned, dropped in another cubelet of ice and a sticky pink cocktail cherry, then presented her with the misted glass. 'Try it,' his raised brows said.

She sipped experimentally and said frankly, 'I'm not a connoisseur, I'm afraid. It – it tastes all right.'

'It isn't the taste, little one, it's the after-affect which is important,' he whispered. 'Come on, we'll sit over there.'

'There' was a cane two-seater definitely constructed only for two. Simon pulled an occasional table conveniently to hand, provided an ashtray, and then settled himself at her side. She cradled her glass in her hands and gazed down into its shimmering circle. Presently Simon said softly: 'Supposing you try looking at me instead. We are not unnoticed.'

Instinctively she glanced at where Della and Johnny had stood and surprised Johnny's speculative stare. It held a trace of surprise and she immediately looked away, this time directly into Simon's inscrutable grey gaze.

One corner of his mouth winged upward. 'That's better. In case you don't know, you are now indulging in the ancient oriental art of face-saving.'

'Whose face?' she asked, after an appreciable pause.

Another smile glimmered. 'You're catching on fast, little one. We won't press that question.'

For some reason Claire came into her thoughts, but she said nothing, taking another sip of her drink. Simon stirred and there was the brief pressure of him against her as he dug down into his pocket for cigarettes. The packet flipped open under her nose, she hesitated. 'I didn't bring any with me – I seem to be smoking all yours.'

'Do two swallows make a . . .?' His brows quirked and he lit two cigarettes and passed one to her. 'See how easy it is if one co-operates?'

'Yes.' She frowned. 'Simon . . .?'

'I don't understand why—'

'Well! Very cosy! Are you two planning to stay there all night?' Johnny stood in front of them, arms akimbo, his eyes alight with mischief. 'Say the word and I'll have the room cleared and the lights out.'

'I'll do my own light-dousing when it's necessary,' Simon said calmly. 'Any more objections?'

Johnny grinned and Della looked down at the younger girl, her smile a little wondering. 'Exchanging your life histories?' she inquired.

'Bored!' said Claire dramatically, appearing suddenly, and her glance was strictly for Simon. 'We've decided to run down to the lake to cool off. It's so sticky tonight I couldn't bear to stay in, but Jason is feeling too lazy to bother so will you drive the Citroen, Simon? It's night time, remember,' she arched roguish brows, 'I'm a menace of a night driver. There'll be room in Drew's car for Venetia, if she wants to come.'

She was turning away with her usual quick brittle movements, as though everything was settled, when Simon said clearly: 'Venetia isn't coming. And you'd better count me out as well.'

'Not coming?' Claire spun on her heel. 'Oh, Simon! But we're all just coming to life! You can't break up the party like that. We're taking the champagne with us, and Kirstie's slipped over to get her radio. It'll be heavenly by the lake side.'

Simon was steadily shaking his head, a faint smile playing round his mouth, and Claire made a visible effort to control her pique. 'It's sheer laziness, Simon. Or has Jason been working you too hard? I must speak to him.'

'I'm here,' said Jason dryly, joining the group. 'What's all this about slave-driving?'

'You should know.'

'Simon's his own boss, and we work in equable harmony. Or do we?'

Simon inclined his head, and Claire flounced round. 'Well, you'll have to come now, Jason. You know I hate driving after dark.'

Jason shrugged, and again there was one of those faintly disturbing exchanges of glances between him and Della. But he went resignedly to get his car keys. There was a concerted exit out to the vehicles, a great deal of laughter and chaffing, and then the sounds of the engines faded.

'Well, I'd better take you home,' Simon said. 'You didn't have a wrap, did you?'

'No.' Without looking at him she descended the verandah steps and strolled on slowly while he closed the door of the Kinlay bungalow and turned off the verandah lights, leaving only the hall light burning. When his steps caught up with her she instinctively quickened her own.

'What's the rush for?'

'Nothing. I'm not rushing.'

'You didn't want to go sparking down by the lake, by any chance?' he asked abruptly, taking her arm.

'Not in the least, but you didn't have to change your plans because of me.'

74

'You don't know what my plans were,' he said calmly, 'so you can get that one out of your head.'

But it had been plain what Claire's had been, she thought, realizing for the first time that evening how significant had been several little things vaguely noticed yet not noticed. She might be imagining that Claire was secretly attracted to Simon Manville, but it wasn't imagination that Claire had every intention of appropriating him as her escort when Jason was otherwise involved. So when Jason cried off it would have worked out entirely to her satisfaction; all the couples neatly paired off, herself casually dismissed, to ride with Drew and Jean Chalmers if she wished, leaving Claire – and Simon.

Venetia was suddenly possessed of righteous indignation; Why should Claire get away with it? She was married, petted and indulged by a thoroughly nice husband, and she still wasn't content. No wonder Jason got fed-up if this was the way Claire behaved. And all those outrageous clothes; didn't she know that the Indian look was as dead as a doornail now in London . . .?

Simon said suddenly: 'What were you going to ask me back there when we were interrupted?'

'I – I don't remember,' she fibbed, after a moment of deliberation. 'It – it wasn't important.'

'You were looking very earnest about it, whatever it was. Have you ever noticed how the time and the place can affect one's choice of conversation?'

'Yes,' she said doubtfully, although she had never given any thought to this particular observation of human behaviour.

'It must have been one of those questions which are easier asked in a brightly lit room amid a crowd of people.'

'Something like that,' she agreed, reflecting that the

question in question was not one she would like to ask Simon Manville in the privacy of the hot scented African night. Politeness might subdue his sardonic sense of humour in the presence of a crowd, but here. . . . All the same, a sense of intrigue persisted and she would dearly love to know why he had made this puzzling *volte-face* regarding herself. He'd previously given her the impression he regarded her as a not very bright child who might prove a nuisance on the landscape any moment. A nuisance he would have to suffer. Now he'd turned all indulgent, almost understanding. Oh, heavens! Surely he wasn't sorry for her, because . . . that would be the crowning indignity. She came to an abrupt halt.

'Simon, you're not sorry for me?' she demanded before second thoughts could stay her tongue.

'Sorry?' There was genuine surprise in his tone as he turned back. 'No, I'm not in the least sorry for you. Thank you.'

It was Venetia's turn to be surprised. 'What for?'

'The compliment.'

She stared suspiciously, trying to read his expression and feeling all her former wariness of him return. Then he put one hand on her shoulder and said gently: 'If you'd thought twice you wouldn't have asked me that, would you? I'm glad you did. I shall be able to eradicate that first unfortunate impression.'

'Oh,' she began to stroll on, not sure that she had successfully sorted out exactly what he meant by that! After a pause, she said slowly, 'What was the second thing?'

'What second thing?'

'When you said that I – Oh, it doesn't matter.'

A slight check of his pace, then, 'I'm glad things have reached that stage already. Do I congratulate myself?'

She stayed silent, aware of becoming inextricably mixed in his riddles and suddenly afraid that he was laughing at her.

He said softly, 'You want to trust me, so why don't you? Listen, I haven't forgotten one single word of our earlier conversation. The question you're too shy to ask is so easily answered, and there's no need of any shame in admission of that answer. Surely you realize that any relationship needs two people to come into parallels of attraction? You picked Johnny; but Johnny didn't pick you. It's as simple as that. But I'll never be able to understand why a woman immediately begins to search for something missing in her make-up – and not the kind you put on your face – and frets herself into misery because the chemistry fails to produce the catalyst she expects.'

'Catalysis negative,' she said flatly.

'Yes, so you cried off the outing this afternoon because you couldn't face it. Pity, you would have enjoyed it. Lizard Rocks is our beauty spot.'

'It'll be something to look forward to, won't it?' she said with commendable lightness, feeling it was high time she steered Simon Manville away from his highly personal analysis of her romantic failings with his closest colleague.

They had reached the gate of the bungalow and she hesitated.

'I'll see you safely in,' he said, motioning her through the gate.

Silently she obeyed, switching on the lights and automatically going to draw the curtains, only to remember that they didn't draw full width because when she bought the material she hadn't known the exact measurements of the window. It made her think of Johnny that day and the comical little discussion they had had in the market, how he had guessed roughly and ordered accordingly. Whatever Simon Manville might say on the subject it still hurt to know that she couldn't attract Johnny. She said tonelessly: 'Would you like a drink?'

'No, thanks.' His mouth looked harder now in the bright light, more the way she had always seen it. 'Are you sure you'll be okay?' he asked. 'The others may not be back for hours.'

'I'll be all right.'

'Not nervous?'

'No.'

'Well, don't take a notion to wander abroad again.'

'I won't.'

'Then I'll say good night.' For an instant he looked down at her, unsmiling, then put out his hand and deliberately tipped up her chin. With the same unhurried deliberation he gripped her shoulder and kissed her, square on the mouth.

His mouth was firm and warm and dry, and when he raised his head and released her she was aware of an un-reasoning sense of anti-climax. Still unsmiling, he stepped back.

'That was just for the practice run,' he said dispassionately. 'It might improve if you let it. Good night.'

She was still standing there, unmoving, when the gate clicked and his steps died into the silence of the night.

CHAPTER FIVE

ONCE again a lull descended on the base after the departure of the visitors. Grumbling ruefully, Della got down to tackling her backlog of work and most of the others seemed conscious of the pressure of work which, if not exactly neglected, had been allowed to slide a little during the past week; only Claire appeared bored and at a loose end amid the sudden onslaught on duty.

But Venetia welcomed it as a respite. She had a great deal to think about and while people were busy they couldn't ask questions or pass observations on the first tentative indications of how relationships were beginning to take form. In the day-to-day intermingling, whether at an informal conference in Admin. or a mid-morning break, or even passing in transit within the base, Johnny seemed to gravitate to Della. Watching the easy camaraderie of them, Venetia could not help thinking of Simon Manville's cool assessment of the situation and unwillingly admitting that it had been accurate. She liked Johnny, Johnny liked his women gay and sophisticated, Della was gay, sophisticated – and very beautiful into the bargain ... the perfect equation, she thought sadly, and one she would have worked out for herself quite easily without help from Simon Manville.

Simon ... Had he been serious that night? That astonishing suggestion about a trial run, a mock flirtation designed to show Johnny that she wasn't exactly languishing alone and unwanted?

Venetia stared at the sheet in the typewriter that was still completely blank except for a tiny winged beetle taking a safari over its virgin surface and tried to decide if she wanted to resort to such devious devices in order to gain any man's attention. The small cold voice of common sense told her that it was extremely unlikely that Johnny would even notice, he was more likely to become even more preoccupied with Della, and, if he did notice, to pull Simon's leg about child-snatching. Little girls! Venetia flicked at the beetle; that crack had stung. She couldn't help it if she wasn't tall and lissom and sexy!

Angrily she typed: *Dear Sire*, and yanked the sheet out, crumpling it and missing the waste-paper basket and shoving in a fresh sheet. Simon Manville had been having a quiet spot of amusement at her expense – it was just the kind of sardonic teasing she might expect from him – and he'd have forgotten all about it by now. Anyway, those silly ideas of playing let's pretend usually ended up with a rebound and a hell of a lot of trouble for everyone concerned – herself! And why had she ever allowed him to catch her off guard with that kiss? *Why*, for that matter, had he delivered that cool, mocking little kiss? There'd been no one to witness it . . .

Oh, forget it, she told herself angrily. Forget that silly coin flip with Della, and a couple of men whose devilry only differed in one respect – one was a fair handsome devil and the other was dark . . .

Thursday had been named as the night of the Great Movie Premiere. The men spent most of the previous evening rigging the screen and sound equipment and essaying a tentative tryout of the film which everyone was strictly forbidden to watch but nevertheless drifted along curiously, to be banished indignantly by Johnny and Mac.

Long before the time advertised in the base news bulletin the audience began to roll down from the big camp by the site of the dam. Whistles, jeers, refreshments strictly of the stern variety, and demands for the traditional cinematic appurtenances were in evidence as the crew jockeyed for advantageous viewpoints.

'Where's the Mighty Wurlitzer?'

'A double in the back row and a jane to go with it, please.'

'Where's the lady with the torchlight?'

'Ice-cream, programmes, cigarettes!' cried a derisive falsetto, and received the instant response: 'You'll be in luck, mate – but the D.D.T.'s on the house!'

A beer can flew through the air, missed the recipient, and a mild scrap broke out, the language turned blue and a derisive howl greeted the appearance of the moon low over the hills beyond the lake.

Venetia moved closer to the screens which sheltered the projection box and wondered wryly if the uproar would cease when the film started. She and Della were supposed to be viewing from the runabout, but Della had forgotten her cigarettes and slipped back to the bungalow for them and Venetia had felt suddenly ill at ease sitting there in the vehicle waiting for something to happen. She heard the muffled tones of Mac from within the box, a sudden staccato burst of sound, and saw the flickering glimmers of silver from the corner of her eye. A cheer almost drowned the soundtrack and she turned hastily in search of Della.

The runabout was still parked a short distance away, and still empty. Surely Della had had time to collect fifty packets of cigarettes! Shrugging, she glanced at the screen and made to climb into the vehicle when a step crunched behind her and a hand closed round her shoulder.

'Well now, you're not sitting this out all lonesome?'

said a voice of metallic raspiness.

Startled, she spun round and met the grinning gaze of the engineer Manville had ejected from the office during that very first week. His eyes raked insolently over her and he grinned again. 'Don't tell me they're neglecting you, my pretty. Come on, up you get.' His hands closed round her waist to lift her into the runabout and a warm reek of spirits came on his breath against her face as he added softly: 'Lucky I was late, eh? I might have—'

'No!' Outrage ousted surprise and Venetia struggled, her small fingers prising against the hot hard hands pinioned about her waist. 'Let go! I—'

'Tch, tch!' he clicked his tongue and laughed softly. 'Fighting! What's the matter? Don't I—'

'You don't! You heard what the lady said. Or maybe you need help.'

There was a confusion of violent movement, very brief, then Venetia was free and the engineer was glaring at the peremptory figure of Simon Manville.

'Scram,' he said briefly 'Unless you'd like to argue.'

For a moment Venetia held her breath. The engineer looked as though he was disposed to argue, and she had never seen Simon look so dangerous. Then the other man glanced at her, grunted something unintelligible, and slouched off into the darkness.

Simon watched him go, then turned to her, the lines of severity softening slightly round his mouth. 'Did he hurt you?'

'No,' she said, a slight tremor shaking her voice, 'I – I just got a bit of a fright. I wasn't expecting him to – Thank you for—'

'Forget it.' He put out one hand, then checked the movement. 'Will you scream if *I* offer you a hand?'

'Of course not! But I can—'

'Don't *you* argue, little one.' Calmly he lifted her as though she were a child and set her on the broad bench seat of the vehicle. His eyes held a glint of mockery as he added, 'I sometimes wonder if the girl of today is trying to kill the spirit of chivalry completely.'

'It depends who offers the chivalry,' she said, looking down at him.

'Granted, but my name isn't Harper, nor do I behave like a whisky-swilling lecher. Or do I?' He turned away and moved round the front of the vehicle to vault in at the other side and seat himself deliberately close to her side. 'Or do I?' he repeated.

'Of course not,' she said helplessly, aware of a sudden tenseness permeating her limbs.

'Then I suggest you relax,' he said dryly, 'and concentrate on this entertainment which has been procured at enormous expense and endeavour.'

'Yes ...' She turned her head a little restlessly, 'but Della hasn't come back.'

'I think your friend is otherwise engaged, and I wouldn't advise a search for her,' he said in the same dry tone.

'Oh.' She tried to fix her gaze on the silver screen, but found it had a strong tendency to stray to the shadowy profile which was much closer. After a moment she felt her hand drawn lightly into the clasp of Simon's. Instinctively she made to free herself and the clasp was instantly withdrawn.

Unaccountably disappointed, she turned her head and met the mocking silvery glints again. He made a small gesture with his hands and dropped them back on his knees. 'My apologies – but I have recollections of what occurs in the back row at the movies. I thought perhaps you'd prefer to know where my hands were.'

Her mouth quivered with exasperated mirth, then stilled

as the cool profile was now presented to her gaze. With a small sigh she put out a groping hand, brushed warm fingers and felt them make their capture. At last she settled back and gave her attention to the film. But somehow, when at last it was over she could recall neither story nor players, nor did it immediately register with her that Johnny had apparently watched the film in the company of Drew Chalmers and of Della there was no sign at all.

*   *   *

'I'll walk you back,' said Simon, 'before I give Mac a hand to put away the gear. Enjoy the film?' he asked as he tucked a companionable hand under her elbow.

'Mm – very much. Burt Reynolds really sends me,' she added with a vague sense of defence.

Simon gave a murmur that could have meant anything and released his grasp for the purpose of lighting a cigarette. He remarked, 'I think you're recovering already.'

'What from?' she asked without thinking.

'If you don't know then you have.' He glanced up at the night sky, now ablaze with a silvery radiance from the ascendant moon. 'By the way, you're not nervous about being alone, are you?'

'Alone?' She stared, and he said impatiently:

'Over the week-end. Or had you forgotten?'

'Oh, yes . . . I mean no, I'm not nervous about being alone while Della's away, if that's what you mean.'

'It is,' he said crisply, 'because if you are I could ask Claire to fix you up for the week-end. They have a spare room.'

'Oh, no,' she said hurriedly, 'I wouldn't want to trouble them. I'll be fine.'

'Good.' He held open the gate and when she had passed through allowed it to swing shut between them. 'See you anon, then.' The briefest of salutes, just a flicker of his hand, and he was loping back along the moonlit road.

Just like that! She stood there, her hands resting on the top of the gate, and stared after him until it became obvious that he wasn't going to glance back or wave. Not quite sure what to think and unconscious of the wry little smile on her lips, she went slowly into the bungalow and for the first time wondered where Della had got to.

She found her friend in front of her dressing-table mirror contemplating nothing in particular.

'Where did you get lost?' she asked.

Della appeared to recall herself. 'I did watch a bit of that flick, but I saw it ages ago, so,' she waved vaguely, 'I decided I'd other more important things to do. You know – for the week-end.'

'Oh . . .' Venetia looked blankly round the bedroom. She could not help noticing that it betrayed few signs of other important things. Usually Della had her room strewn with clothes and accessories whenever she was preparing to go away, even if only for one night. 'You don't seem to be making much progress,' she said bluntly.

'Eh? Oh, I shan't take much.'

Della lapsed back into silence and Venetia stared at her friend. Della wasn't usually so – she searched for the right word – evasive. After an appreciable pause she asked, 'You all right, Della?'

'Me? I'm fine! I haven't turned grey overnight, or – or grown horns or something, have I?'

'No, of course you haven't.' Venetia turned away. There had been the suggestion of an edge to Della's tone which had jarred instantly, and even though Venetia was aware of her own sensitivity that tended to colour her imagination she knew she wasn't being either imaginative or touchy. She was about to go from the room when Della turned round and smiled.

'Did I sound snappy? Sorry, pet, but I was thinking something out.'

'It's okay,' said Venetia, 'I'll leave you to it.'

'Sorry,' Della said again. 'By the way, before I forget . . . Jason asked me to tell you to just wander along to their place any time over the week-end if you get lonesome.'

Jason . . . Venetia raised her brows. 'Everybody seems to be worrying in case I get lonesome this week-end.'

'You shouldn't be so popular.'

'I didn't know I was.' For a moment Venetia verged on launching into an account of the evening and the incident with the unpleasant Harper, then she changed her mind and bade her friend good night. It was obvious that Della had something on her mind, and for no valid reason she could pin down Venetia felt vaguely uneasy. *Where* had Della been this evening? And why had she suddenly become so secretive?

However, Della appeared to have got over her preoccupation by the following morning, to the extent of immediately spotting an air of languor about Venetia.

'You look a bit under the weather this morning, my pet. All right?'

'Just a bit of a headache,' Venetia said. 'I'll take some aspirins. It'll go off later.'

But even after the aspirins the headache did not go off, nor did the heavy shadows fade from under her eyes. The feeling of malaise persisted all day and with it a strong disinclination to eat. Noting Della's occasional glances of concern, she made an effort to appear her normal self and to answer lightly when Della, preparing to depart with Johnny, voiced another comment of Venetia's pallor.

Aware of Johnny hovering impatiently, Venetia hissed:

'Can't you tell? I'm green! Seasick! It's sheer envy!'

'So that's it! Sure?' Della did not look entirely convinced. However, she whispered back: 'Well, look after yourself – and get some warpaint on to disguise that haggard envy.'

Claire was also hovering. She chipped in: 'I think Ven's going under the heat. Not everyone can take it. Don't worry, we'll keep an eye on her,' she added casually.

Suddenly Venetia wished they would all leave her alone. But there was no escaping Claire's insistence that she 'drop in' that evening and they would plan something for the week-end.

Back at the bungalow she told Tobi she wanted neither tea nor an evening meal and to his surprised: 'Missy all right?' said she was eating out. When he had departed she took some aspirins and flopped limply on her bed; if anyone else asked if she was all right or announced they were going to keep an eye on her she would scream. The only plans she wanted to make for the week-end revolved round getting rid of this infernal headache and certain other unpleasant symptoms which had manifested themselves. Pray God she wasn't going to distinguish herself by falling prey to some ghastly tropical malady before she'd been here more than five minutes. Thank heaven it was a week-end and Della was away. She'd make an excuse of something – anything – and keep out of everyone's way, and by Monday and Della's return she'd be okay.

At eight o'clock she dragged herself wearily off the bed and showered and changed, talcuming herself liberally in an effort to cool her hot, irritable body, and set off reluctantly for the Kinlay bungalow, aghast at the feeling of weakness that seemed to increase with every step.

On the veranda she hesitated, almost inclined to turn and give in to the longing to flee. But it was too late; Jason had spotted her and called a friendly, 'Come in.'

'Didn't you know that when the door's left open you just walk in?' He poured her a drink and raised his brows when she asked hastily if she could have fruit juice only. 'No sorrows to drown?' he quizzed, returning the Gordon's to the tray.

'Mine are all good swimmers,' she said wryly.

He laughed, the jug of fruit juice in his hand. 'Would you like a Campari?'

'No, thanks.' She sank in a chair and managed a smile. 'It's beautifully cool in here and dim.'

'I'm afraid it won't be like that for long when Claire comes in and lights up. I like the air-conditioning practically down to freezing, I'm afraid. I think Claire and I have different built-in thermostat settings.'

After a pause she suddenly asked: 'You can adjust the air-conditioning? I mean will ours adjust in our bungalow?'

'Good gracious, yes.' Jason seemed surprised. 'Haven't you two found how it works yet?'

'I never gave it a thought,' she admitted.

'Come, I'll show you,' he offered. 'There'll be a control like this set in a panel in the recess beside your icebox. You adjust it like this to the degree you find most comfortable – you'll have to experiment. And there's a control in each room to cut it off or on as you require.'

'I didn't know. Thank you,' she said, glad now that she had come after all, or she might still have been in ignorance of this comfort.

'I'm surprised one of the boys didn't think to put you wise,' Jason said, returning with her to the lounge and mixing himself another drink. He glanced at the large sheaf of papers spread on a side table and said absently, 'I wonder where Claire's got to.'

Venetia stayed silent. Without wishing to be bitchy in any way she found Jason much more relaxing company than his wife. At the best of times Claire was exhausting, and this was anything but one of the best times. She sipped at her drink and decided that the headache had abated slightly, which was probably because of the dim, cool room. She glanced up and saw that Jason was standing by the table, leaning on outspread hands and frowning down at the big blueprint. On the wall was pinned a large map, a duplicate of the one which hung in his office, and after a moment he raised his head and scratched absently at his chin as he frowningly contemplated a point on the map.

Venetia stirred uneasily, wondering if she disturbed him, and set her empty glass silently on the small coffee table. Maybe she ought to go. It looked as though Claire had got involved elsewhere. She started to rise and Jason turned.

'I'm sorry, Ven, I'm not making you very welcome. I don't—'

'No,' she said quickly, 'you're busy and I'm disturbing you. I'll—'

He smiled. 'You don't disturb me, child, but you didn't come here to sit and stare at a reminder of work. I wonder if Claire's gone to sleep in the hammock. I'll go and see.'

'No, don't bother. I'll go and find her if I may.'

'Tell her I've drunk all the gin – that'll fetch her,' said Jason with a wry grin.

The garden at the rear of the bungalow stretched quite a distance and had been well laid out with flowering shrubs and equipped with garden furniture. Claire's hammock had been slung in a shady spot about halfway down, and Venetia wandered slowly down the path by the oleander hedge. But the big striped hammock was empty, a couple of magazines lying in it and an empty glass in which several insects had already drowned in the sticky dregs were the only traces of its recent occupation.

Venetia turned away, feeling the perspiration clammy at her temples and the uncomfortable sensation of her dress clinging to her irritable skin. The night seemed even hotter than ever, and walking out of the coolness indoors was like penetrating an invisible wall of heat. She would slip away, Claire had forgotten about her, she would see her some time over the week-end . . . better not disturb Jason . . .

She had traversed about half the distance to the side gate when she heard Claire's voice quite close by. Coming immediately to the conclusion that Claire had missed her, she took a hasty step forward and opened her lips to announce her whereabouts. But her voice did not come and her step checked as she heard the end snatch of what Claire was saying and the deep voice which responded.

Simon! Not Jason!

Venetia desperately wanted to duck and move back, but for some reason the sound and presence of Simon Manville seemed to have the effect of paralysing her limbs. She heard Claire laugh scornfully, and Simon say quite clearly: 'I don't believe it, you're imagining things, Claire.'

'Naturally, you men always stick together.'

'Yes, but Jason . . .'

'And why not Jason? Do you think he's immune?' Claire's voice was husky and vibrant through the scented darkness. 'Is any man immune, always? Are you, Simon?'

Venetia stifled a groan. This was dreadful, she *had* to escape. But she couldn't, they were just a little way ahead and if she stirred they would hear, see the pale blur of her dress moving. . . . She tried to close her ears, close every sense, but Simon Manville's low urgent tones penetrated as though she were a microphone, picking up and amplifying every nuance, and vivid mental visions of him filled her mind. His hands would be on Claire's shoulders, would be making the only gesture possible as he said forcefully:

'Listen, Claire, for God's sake don't! You'll only succeed in—'

'Ruining everything? I know, the favourite male cliché. I don't want to wait, Simon. What will I ruin? Do you think Jason cares a damn? I see no reason why I should. In fact I'm glad it's happened. It's going to make a certain difference to one problem, at least.'

'It can't, and you know it,' he said tersely. 'You're hurt, Claire, it's natural, but you can't possibly be serious.'

'Serious? Darling, I've never been so serious in my life. Listen, Simon, I've suspected it all along; for nearly two years, ever since she came, and now I'm sure.' Claire's voice quickened and a hint of viciousness sharpened it. 'Why do you think he was so determined to have her out here? And as for this other affair . . . of course it's all a blind, but if they think for one moment I'm fooled . . .'

'I still think you're mistaken, reading too much into a couple of incidents.' But the deep voice did not carry complete conviction and Claire said angrily:

'Then why did she cut out the other kid? No, she needs Johnny, and really, it's pathetic the way that kid lights up when he comes within half a mile.'

'So I've noticed,' said Simon dryly.

'It stuck out a mile that night we had the crowd here – she was brokenhearted. Why do you think she cried off the trip to Lizard Rock?' Claire paused, then laughed softly. 'But you know, Simon, you don't have to play the shining knight so assiduously, you might find yourself with her on your conscience at the finish.'

'I don't think that's likely.'

'I wouldn't like to bet on it, but still, she doesn't really come into it. Heavens!' Claire seemed to recollect something, 'she's coming along tonight. We'd better go indoors. Oh, Simon, I'm glad I've told you. I had to have someone and I'd rather it was you, as we—'

The voice faded and the soft brushing sounds of Claire's skirt against the feathers of fern bordering the path, her exclamation at some unseen impediment, and the faint resonance of Simon's response.

For long moments of shocked immobility Venetia could grasp only one dreadful realization; they were talking about Della! They believed Della and Jason were ... Della and Jason ... Della and Jason ... The appalling accusation hammered through her brain, reiterating endlessly as she stumbled away from the Kinlay bungalow and made her way blindly along the road. It couldn't be true! Della had gone off for the week-end with Johnny. She wouldn't go off with one man if she was in love with another. But Claire believed that was a blind ... that Della was using Johnny so that she – so that she and Jason ...

Reaction set in when Venetia reached her own place. She was trembling as though with an ague and her body burned with dry fire. It took ages to assemble the things to make herself a cup of tea and find some plain biscuits that stuck in her mouth like choking pieces of cardboard. She took more aspirins and made herself drink the tea, subconsciously aware that she must have fluid, and all the time the questions pounded through her head, drumming in unholy alliance with the throbbing pain making renewed onslaught at her temples. Was it true? There were all the small things vaguely noticed that now flowered to frightening new fears. Della had been preoccupied of late. Where had she gone the previous evening during the film show? Where had she been on a couple of other occasions when Venetia had missed her? The base wasn't the kind of place where one could disappear for any length of time without bumping into someone. It was, in fact, one of the most unprivate places Venetia had known, the only two people who lived in quarters unshared were Dr. Vanders – and Simon.

She mustn't think of Simon, of the scathing little 'I *don't think that's likely*' that had inflicted an unexpected sting. It was Della she had to worry about. Claire had made a dreadful mistake. Della would never dream of becoming involved with a married man. But she couldn't forget that sense of *rapport*, a strange kind of intimate understanding between Della and her boss, shared glances that conveyed so much . . .

Miserably confused, Venetia made herself go round the bungalow closing the screens securely. She found the control Jason had told her about and turned down the setting, then stumbled back to bed, to huddle beneath the thin sheet and try to ignore pain spasms that drew her knees up to her chest in instinctive recoil. The band of her pyjamas seemed too tight, even though the elastic was quite slack, and there seemed no comfortable resting position. And she had left the hall light burning . . . what did it matter? Della wasn't here. The slightest chink of light anywhere kept Della awake . . . was Della having an affair with Jason? She would have to warn her . . . tell that Claire knew, and . . .

The pains subsided a little and Venetia dozed uneasily, first huddled into a small cramped ball, then stretched taut to her full length, then limp, her limbs spreadeagled untidily. . . . She woke once, with a raging thirst, and raised

93

herself to drink greedily from the glass on the bedside locker. Was it only midnight? If only the long dark night were over. . . . Her head drooped on the rumpled pillow, and her wide eyes stared at the bright chink of light under the door. She should get up and switch off that light . . . but a kind of stupor wouldn't allow her to make the effort to try . . . or move when she heard the crunch of footsteps on the path outside. If an intruder were to break in she couldn't do a thing about it. . . . But the intruder called her name . . . it wasn't an intruder . . . she'd left the lights on and Simon Manville was checking up on her, asking if she was awake . . . asking if she was all right . . .

'Yes, I'm all right. I – I—' her voice sounded thin and dull in her own ears and he would never hear it, and oh! – even Simon Manville's proximity brought a sense of salvation. She raised herself on one elbow and the movement brought a rush of clammy weakness and nausea. Her face crumpled and she cried with the despair of fright: 'No, Simon, I'm not all right, I'm – I feel as though – Simon, *please don't go away!*'

There was a moment of astounded silence, then hurrying feet and a door slamming.

'Venetia!' Light flooded the room, so dazzling it blinded her. 'What the—!' He took a step forward, his face dark with alarm, and half turned, almost questing of the atmosphere in the room. 'But this place is like a glacier!'

'Is it?'

'It most certainly is.' He came to the bedside, looked down at her flushed face, and laid one hand lightly over her forehead. 'How long have you been like this?'

'Since last night – no, tonight. At least, that is, this morning. I—'

'All right, you can tell me in a moment. Where are the blankets?'

'In a cupboard somewhere, I – I think.'

With an impatient movement he took off his jacket and put it over her. He went from the room and returned with the coverlet from Della's bed. He folded it double and added it to the jacket. 'What possessed you to turn the air-conditioning to zero?'

'I was too hot, and I didn't know you could adjust it until Jason told me how.'

'What have you eaten?'

'Nothing,' she shook her head wearily. 'I couldn't.'

'Much alcohol?'

'No!' Weak indignation strengthened the negative.

'Headache?'

She nodded.

He touched her forehead again. 'I think you've got a bit of a temperature. Been rushing to the bathroom?'

She turned her face into the pillow and he made a small impatient gesture. 'There's no need to be embarrassed, little one. We've all suffered it at some time or other. It's all the same – gippy tummy, or what Johnny calls T.T.T. – tropic travellers' trot. Any sickness?'

'Not yet.'

His mouth compressed as he regarded her for a few moments, then he said decisively: 'I'm going to bring Muriel along to check you, just to be on the safe side. I won't be very long.'

'No!' she put out a hand to stay him. 'I don't want a doctor. I – I think Della has some stuff she brought with her just in case we – we got any upsets. I'll find it and take some, and . . .' she looked at him imploringly, 'please don't bring Dr. Vanders.'

'Why not?'

'It can't be very serious, and she might – I don't want to be a nuisance.'

'There's no question of you being a nuisance. That's why she's here, and why we have a fully equipped dispensary. To take care of upsets like this.'

The mention of the dispensary brought terror to Venetia's face, and Simon frowned. 'Surely you're not scared of going in for a little while until you've pulled round? It's the only way. You can't stay here alone.'

'No,' she said stubbornly, 'if I'm ill and it takes a bit to – to get better they might send me home, and I – I don't want to—'

'What nonsense! Not another word. Now don't you move until I get back. Promise?'

She nodded dumbly, and lay palpitating under the covers he had put over her, still not sure that Dr. Vanders wouldn't take one look at her and promptly decide to invalid her home. And Dr. Vanders would want to examine her, and she'd find . . . Venetia drew in a breath that was agitated and wished she'd never given in to that moment of weakness when she'd called Simon . . .

But when he returned he was alone.

'Muriel's gone to the camp – one of the men has a suspected dislocation of his shoulder. That's one sensible thing about Muriel,' he added, 'she always leaves a message on the slate to say where she is. So I've left word and she'll be down to see you as soon as she can. In the meantime, I'm to make you as comfortable as possible.'

He proceeded to mix a small dose of medicine from a bottle he had brought from the dispensary, made her drink it, then said briskly, 'Now if you could sit up for a minute or so we'll straighten that bed and sponge your face.'

'Oh.' She clutched the coverlet and stared at him

doubtfully. Quite obviously he was misreading the reason for her reluctance, and she added hurriedly: 'I – I don't think you should touch me. I – I think I'm – infectious!'

'Infectious!' Simon betrayed the first sign of astonishment. 'Whatever idea have you got into that frightened little head now, for heaven's sake? Infectious?'

'No.' Her mouth trembled ominously. She might have guessed he wouldn't take her seriously. 'I've got a *rash*,' she whispered, as though it were some dreadful guilty secret she was confessing, and waited for the instant revulsion she was fully prepared to see in his face.

Instead, he merely raised his brows. 'So you've got a rash. I don't see any sign of one.'

'No, it hasn't spread that far yet.'

'How far *has* it spread?' He did not appear in the least bit concerned, though there was a hint of watchfulness in his eyes.

'It's on my back and – and—' she licked dry lips, 'it's very irritable.'

'Is it?' He made a small grimace of casual concern. 'Well, do you think you could bring yourself to let me see this awful eruption? I've an idea what it might be, but I can't tell unless . . .'

After a long contemplation of his grave expression she sighed and wriggled over on to her stomach, and hitched up the back of her pyjama jacket a few cautious inches.

There was no immediate expelled breath of disgust and she manoeuvred one hand upwards in vague indication. 'It's round there somewhere, I know.'

Dispassionately he reached down and yanked the pyjama jacket free till it was gathered in concertina folds over the back of her head. 'Oh, yes, I see now,' he said in disinterested tones. 'Yes, definitely a rash. I should say your days are numbered now, little one.'

'What?' She struggled under the muffling folds of material and started up. 'Is it – it isn't really something dreadful . . .?'

'No!' Gently he drew down the crumpled pink lawn and smiled, his face softening. 'It's only heat rash, little one, and it's confined to where I expected it to be – round the waistline and where your bra straps rest. Does it reach round the front as well?'

She nodded, still not completely convinced, and he said, 'Don't worry, I'll fetch some cream to put on which will soothe it and prevent any further infection, but you'll have to avoid wearing anything tight until it clears, because it could develop into something nasty.'

'Is it prickly heat?' she asked.

He nodded. 'It's very common in hot climates, but not exactly fatal.'

'I think half of this has been sheer fright, hasn't it?' he said when he returned again a few minutes later after his second raid on Dr. Vanders' medical store. 'You've heard so many tales of the dire afflictions in the tropics you imagined the worst.'

'Mm, a bit like that, I think,' she murmured against the pillow, and at last began to feel a little more relaxed. The cream he was applying was deliciously cool and soothing – or was it the firm yet surprisingly gentle hands that brought peace and a warm pervading sense of comfort? 'Here,' the tube of cream descended on the pillow beside her, 'you can do the front yourself while I fix a warm drink for you.'

A little drowsy now, she completed the application of cream and wriggled more comfortably into her pyjama jacket. Dear Simon; what would she have done without him? The long dark night no longer loomed miserable and endless before dawn, and the sick secret fears were retreating to their horrible lairs. How mistaken one could be about people, she thought suddenly, listening to the friendly, reassuring sounds that drifted from the direction of the kitchen. Until tonight Simon Manville was the last person she would have called for in emergency – this kind of emergency! – and the last man she would have credited capable of the calm, gentle administrations with which he was tending her.

When he came back with the tray he gave her the big beaker of weak milky tea and settled himself with his drink in the cane chair by the window. Somehow there was a settled look about the way he composed his long legs and she said guiltily:

'It must be terribly late and you've been twice across to the dispensary and—'

'It's practically next door.' He shrugged.

'Yes, but . . . you must be terribly tired.'

'Not as tired as you look. Think you'll sleep now?'

'Oh, yes, I'll be fine now, but I've kept you all this time, and—'

'Go to sleep.'

'Yes, but . . .'

'I'm not going until you're settled, and I don't think you're capable at the moment of throwing me out, so you may as well obey orders for once.'

He uncurled himself lazily and took the beaker away, then switched out the light and asked: 'Shall I leave the small lamp on?'

'Yes, please.' She looked up at him from under shadowing lashes and thought inconsequently how tall he looked from this angle. There was the suggestion of a smile lurking round his mouth and she said doubtfully, 'Are you going now?'

He shook his head. 'Just go to sleep. I won't be very far

away.'

'Oh.' She digested this, too tired to argue any more and aware of the clouds of sleep hovering very near. Yet she knew a reluctance to succumb and let her drooping eyelids close. She sighed again. 'Thanks for coming and – and everything.'

'Go to sleep.' The smile quivered again and a light touch of hard knuckles brushed against her cheek. 'There's just one other thing,' he added in exactly the same inflection, 'in case you're worrying. That practice run . . . we'd better leave it in neutral territory, for a little while.'

CHAPTER SIX

A SURPRISED Della arrived back late on Sunday evening to find Venetia ensconced in Dr. Vanders' quarters adjoining the dispensary building.

'You know, I thought you looked under the weather last Friday before I left,' she said when she had got over the initial discovery extravagances. 'If I'd known it was as bad as this I'd have cancelled the trip.'

'That was what I was afraid of,' said Venetia.

Della gave a small exclamation. 'You poor pet, and when I was going off with ... and instead you've been stuck in here since Saturday. You poor pet,' she repeated ruefully.

'Actually, I've quite enjoyed myself. Muriel's great fun when you get to know her, and Noni — that's the Ethiopian girl who is going to be Muriel's nursing sister at the new clinic — arrived on Saturday to start her new job, she'll be staying here until they move over to Noyali in three weeks' time — kept me company. She's awfully sweet, so you see it hasn't been anything like I was afraid of.'

As she made this pronouncement Venetia was discovering that it *was* true; she *had* enjoyed herself, and by the Saturday night she had recovered to the point of feeling like a fraud. She saw the trace of disbelief on Della's face and said: 'It's true, I have, honestly. It was the best way, actually. Muriel wanted to run some tests on me, just to be certain I hadn't picked up anything serious, and it wasn't practical for me to stay alone in the bungalow.'

Della eyed the bowl of massed blooms and the assortment of magazines on the table, the transistor radio by the bed and the sewing laid carelessly on the gay coloured cushions in one chair, and wrinkled her nose. 'You seem to be cosy enough, but it still smells like a hospital – gives me the creeps.'

Venetia smiled and took up the sewing. 'It doesn't worry me.'

'It's still a shame,' Della sighed. 'You won't have had that fun week-end with Simon after all.'

Venetia blinked. 'What did you say? What fun week-end with . . .?'

'Well, I don't know, pet. I thought . . .' Della hesitated, giving a vague gesture.

Venetia sat up sharply and clutched at the arms of her chair. 'You thought what?' she asked, unaware of the demand in the straining of her body. 'What about Simon and a fun week-end?'

'Darling, don't look so fierce! It was just that while we were away I was a bit worried about you and I happened to remark once to Johnny that I hoped you were okay, and he said, "Oh, don't worry, I think Simon's planning to take care of her this week-end."'

'Oh.' Venetia sat back.

'So I guess they must talk about us,' Della grinned. 'So of course I wondered . . . but he couldn't do much about it if you were ill, could he, pet?'

'No,' said Venetia.

There was a pause, then Della asked, 'Have you seen him at all?'

'Yes.' Venetia frowned absently at the sewing in her lap. Yes, she had seen Simon, and taken up quite a lot of his time, even though not by the wildest stretch of imagination could the week-end have been termed 'fun'. All the same, she retained several memories in which Simon figured rather largely and which for the moment she had an absurd reluctance to share with anyone – even Della. A faint smile curved her mouth. She was almost certain he had spent the rest of that night on the settee in the lounge – that ridiculously small cane settee for his long frame – he couldn't have got any rest! – because she'd had a kind of dream that someone had looked in on her, as though to make sure she slept peacefully, but it hadn't been the scarey sort of dream at all, and she'd turned over and realized she was half awake, then she'd slept again and the next thing she knew Simon was waking her at half past seven.

He'd told her that Dr. Vanders would probably be along by eight, and he'd taken over as calmly and firmly as when he'd first arrived. By the time Muriel came she'd had a very light breakfast, the first food she'd felt like eating for two days, and had managed to tidy her hair and look a little more human. Muriel had given her a quick check and provisionally confirmed Simon's surmise as to the cause of the trouble. Nevertheless, Muriel had insisted on her adjourning to the dispensary for the rest of the week-end, pending results of the tests she wanted to run.

Simon had said promptly that the order would be obeyed and after Muriel had gone Venetia had got up to dress. The woolliness of her legs had shocked her – she'd got as far as the door and wondered if she would make it as far as the tourer Simon had brought to the gate. He'd put her small case in the tourer and come back for her, to shake his head impatiently and exclaim, 'Rubber knees!' as he picked her up in his arms. She had giggled weakly, conscious of the world tilting crazily as he came through the doorway into the brilliant morning. Then he'd stopped abruptly, to close the door behind them, and instead of setting her down again he had said in that indulgent, exasperated tone, 'You don't try to be a very co-operative patient, do you? Lost the use of your hands?' Unexpectedly he had loosened his hold with one arm and to save herself from falling she'd had to grab round his neck. . . . His shoulders had felt rock-hard, yet warm and safe to cling to, and she could still feel the shoulder seam of his shirt press into the skin of her arm, remember wriggling slightly where the sharp corner of something in his breast pocket dug into her. There had been the faintest shadow of beard on the tanned jawline so close to her face, and the tang of the stuff he used on his hair mingling with the clean masculine smell that was just . . . just him and no one else in the world. When that small journey was over the weakness in her knees seemed to have spread to the rest of her . . .

She became aware of Della staring sharply at her and of the annoying warmth that had crept into her cheeks during that sojourn into retrospect. She said hastily: 'Did *you* have a good time?'

'Wonderful! We brought a small token back for you, but I didn't bring it as I haven't unpacked yet. How much longer will it be before you escape?'

'Tomorrow, I hope. But Jason said I had to take the rest of the week off. I won't know what to do with myself,' she sighed.

'Lazy little wretch,' said Della affectionately. 'I bet you've been pandered to. Who brought in the herbaceous border?' she nodded towards the enormous bowl of flowers.

'Jason – this morning. He said it was like bringing coals to Newcastle, but I'm not allowed titbits and he said he'd never claimed to be an original person.'

'Pity they're dying already.' Della got up and crossed to the table, to bend over and touch the blossoms with a gesture that was oddly lingering.

Venetia's gaze took on the sharpness of worry as she thought of the unpleasant warning she had to give Della. It was a task she did not relish but which she would have to face. She opened her lips, then closed them; it was going to be more difficult than she had anticipated. How on earth did she start to recount that conversation and the accusation Claire had unmistakably conveyed? Supposing she had got it wrong, that Claire had been speaking of some other mutual acquaintance? It could be possible, though Venetia knew in her heart that she had not jumped to erroneous conclusions.

While she tried to formulate the right approach Della straightened and announced that she must make trek, and Venetia suddenly knew she could not bring herself to impart the sordid little tale – not yet. She would wait until she was back in home quarters and the right mood presented itself for the making of confidences. Yes, she would wait a little while . . .

Later, she was to wish with all her heart she hadn't.

It was Tuesday afternoon before Dr. Vanders at last gave the okay to 'filter back into circulation' and with a sigh of thankfulness Venetia lost no time in commencing to 'filter'. The ennui tropical Africa could induce came insidiously and she had had quite enough of trying to fill in three long empty days with inactivity. Della was openly delighted to have her back, admitting frankly that she wasn't the kind of self-sufficient person who could live happily alone . . . 'I was surprised how quiet the place was,' she remarked the following morning, 'especially at breakfast time.'

Venetia nodded, immediately aware of the unconscious inference; Della's evenings would never be lonely. She sighed, remembering her own disappointment the previous evening when Johnny had arrived – alone. He'd carried

Della off for an evening drive and it had been long after eleven when they returned. To be fair, they'd asked her if she would like to accompany them, and naturally they had assumed that her instant refusal was due to not yet being completely recovered from her illness, and it didn't even occur to her that they might surmise she was still suffering from heart-burnings over Johnny himself. Somehow she had been so certain that Simon would call in, even if only for a fleeting visit, but he didn't, and her only visitor was Claire, who brought a couple of books, chatted a little while in a bored, desultory fashion, then departed soon after volunteering the information that Simon had gone off for a couple of days; another conference.

She found she was wishing he had told her – but why should he? she asked herself, aware of how unsatisfactory an answer the little question proved.

The week dragged on, the old routine gradually establishing itself, and by the Friday the disruption of the previous week-end was already being enclosed in memory like a small island of sand being isolated, then covered by the incoming tide.

Several times the worrying thought of Claire's insinuation returned to nag at her, and each time she wondered how to best to broach it, but as the days passed with apparently unruffled calm it became more easy to dismiss it as an incident which had been too highly coloured by her own imagination. Johnny was possessive, almost proprietorial towards Della – there couldn't possibly be any opportunity for her to indulge in secret assignations with Jason. And Jason himself, apparently as imperturbable behind that calm air of authority, was spending a great deal of time at the construction site, where so far Della had not been required to accompany him during the course of her working hours, an omission which apparently had not occurred to her to date. Then suddenly it did.

'You know,' she remarked idly on the Friday evening after the weekly film show was over, 'I'm beginning to think we're fated to return home after living six months almost within sight of it without even seeing the damn thing.'

Jason shuddered at the awful pun and said mildly, 'If you're willing to risk breaking your ankle and getting smothered in dust then by all means go and inspect it.'

'You were the one who banned our presence there,' Della reminded him.

'I should think so,' said Claire. 'The official opening will be quite soon enough for me.'

There was a short silence, then Johnny said, 'Well, you've only to say the word, ladies, and I'll be delighted to act as escort.'

For a moment no one seemed disposed to accept the offer, which was patently addressed only to one young lady in particular, then Simon glanced at the silent Venetia and raised his brows. 'Not interested?'

'Of course!' she exclaimed, trying to convey indignation at an accusation of lack of interest and at the same time not betray indignation that he'd taken all this time to deign to notice her presence. All the evening she'd sought some indication of the brief tenderness and understanding she'd glimpsed in him during that disquieting night exactly one week ago and so far it had not been forthcoming. Now she was beginning to wonder if she'd been half delirious that night and imagined it all. 'Of course I'm interested,' she asserted in a cool little voice. 'I'd very much like to see the dam being built.'

'Then you shall.' His glance was equally cool and off-hand. 'We'll go on Sunday.'

'How about us?' said Johnny to Della.

Before she could reply Claire said suddenly: 'Why don't we all go? We could make a jaunt out of it. And we could take the gear and have a barbecue at Lizard Rocks afterwards. Anyway,' she added sweetly, 'I think it's time I showed up this rival for my husband's affection.'

'It would be a bit of an armful,' Johnny grinned.

'And a cold one,' said Simon dryly.

'I wouldn't be sure of that,' Claire said, with a smile that didn't quite reach her eyes and a glance at Della that was fleeting enough for Venetia to wonder if it had held the venom the words had. 'Well,' Claire added, 'is it on?'

Somewhat to Venetia's disappointment, the idea was seized on with enthusiasm by the others, with the exception of Jason, who remarked that he'd never enjoyed mixing work with pleasure but he'd try for a special occasion, and the outing was planned there and then.

Wisely, the girls dressed sensibly for the occasion in light slacks and shirts and flatties, although at the last moment Venetia was tempted to don more dressy attire when she remembered Simon issuing a pointed little warning about not turning up dressed for Ascot. Did he think she was too dense to heed Jason's remark about dust and broken ankles?

But when the party assembled early on the Sunday morning it was obvious that Claire at least had no intention of letting a bit of dust inhibit her dress sense. She sauntered up to them, swinging her tote bag and fully aware of the attractive picture she presented. Venetia eyed the dazzling white, very brief-fitting shorts that revealed long tanned legs, the tiny button-up matching tunic top, the flaring cover-up jacket of tailored white with red polka dots, the piratical neckerchief over shining silvery tresses that completed the ensemble, and felt like a cobber down on the farm beside the poised older girl.

'Next stop Miami beach?' said Johnny, eyeing Claire's legs appreciatively, and Claire gave him an arch glance.

'I said I was going to show up this rival, didn't I?' she said lightly. 'Who's going with who?'

'We'll take Dr. Vanders and Noni,' said Jason, 'and the rest will sort itself out.'

It was already doing that, as Mac and Drew Chalmers were stowing themselves and the picnic gear in the Land Rover and Johnny, with Della at his side, was revving up the runabout.

'Come on, Miss last-as-usual.' Simon indicated the tourer, and after a brief hesitation Venetia got into the front passenger seat.

'I'm not always last,' she protested when he got in beside her. 'Anyway, the tortoise got there in the end and had time to see the scenery on the way.'

'I wasn't referring exactly to time and motion,' he said, slipping into gear and moving slowly forward to give the dust in the wake of the preceding vehicle time to settle.

'Then what were you referring to?' She fished her sunglasses out of her pocket and put them on, then sat back and stared straight ahead.

'One day it might dawn, in the meantime, you continue to study the scenery, little one,' he said dryly. 'You'll probably be happier that way.'

Venetia gave a small sigh and an expressive glance heavenwards; he was in one of his enigmatic moods this morning, obviously. Well, if he didn't want to spell it out ... But she could not resist stealing a sidelong glance and discovered the sardonic grin that was lurking round his mouth. She said tartly: 'The scenery seems to find something funny about it, anyway.'

The smile flickered, and was brought under control. 'The scenery is concentrating on the road at the moment, but it won't be occupied indefinitely, remember.'

'Is that another warning?' she asked after a brief pause.

'That depends on the way *you* look at it.'

'Oh.' Venetia decided it was time to concentrate on the more conventional scenery unfolding with the passing landscape – it didn't answer back, unless one counted the raucous birdlife that flashed in vivid colourful flight from the oncoming vehicle.

The track was winding through the heart of the forest now and the dense tangle of lush vegetation on each side seemed to hint at mysteries dark and concealed. Secret stirrings that stilled the moment the eye sought to hold them, as though they waited for the intruder to pass before resuming the ceaseless busyness of nature at its most primitive.

Presently the forest thinned to a clearing, in the centre of which towered the biggest tree Venetia had ever seen. Ancient, decayed, its only life that of the lichen and creeper bound about its vast bulk, a great hollow cleft its base and formed an aperture large enough into which to drive a car. Simon slowed, noticing her interest, and started to speak, then stopped to raise his hand with a casual wave.

At the far side of the clearing the runabout stood, and Della and Johnny were sitting on a fallen log beneath the monstrous tree. Johnny's arm was round Della's shoulders and he held a can of lager in his free hand while Della was attempting to master the art of drinking from a can and laughing too much to succeed.

'Do we pick you up on the way back?' Simon called.

'You do your own picking up, mate,' Johnny shouted back, and Della added a remark which was lost in his more stentorian voice.

Simon grinned and drove on, to halt under the shade of a cool dark eucalyptus grove. He reached into the capacious map compartment and produced a couple of cans. 'Ready for refreshments?'

'Yes, please.'

'Lime or Coke?'

'Oh, either. You have which you want.'

'I'm having something a little less cloying.' He opened the lime juice, produced a straw from the cache under the dashboard, and handed it to her, then sorted out his own drink.

After a couple of mouthfuls he said casually: 'Does it still hurt, little one?'

She knew that the recent small encounter prompted the question and said truthfully: 'No, not now.'

'Good.' He took another leisurely swig and contemplated the can as though mentally measuring the contents yet remaining. 'Do you think you're sufficiently recovered to resume that practice run?'

'I'm quite recovered.' She carefully straightened the top of her straw. 'But there isn't any need now for – for a practice run.'

'I'm not sure about that. I mean, how else do you announce to to the world that it doesn't hurt any more?'

'I hadn't quite thought of it from that angle.'

He turned and tossed the empty can into the back of the car. 'I guessed you hadn't, and' – he started the engine and gave her a long direct look – 'you're going to be awful lonesome.'

She stared at him. 'Am I?'

He nodded. 'If you stay odd girl out.'

Three miles farther on they reached the new settlement area.

Venetia emerged from her silence to merge with the others as they looked at the rows of neat little white dwellings, each with its own plot for growing vegetables and entitlement to a strip of land on the fertile hillside overlooking the settlement. Nearby was the new clinic and child welfare centre of which Dr. Vanders was to be in charge. With Noni at her side she showed them round its sparkling clinical interior and proudly explained the functions of the well-equipped laboratory and treatment rooms.

There was also a school, not yet completed, and the gaunt shell of what would grow into a community centre, and a little farther on the partially constructed highway which would link the new Noyali township to Mortonstown. They were all rather thoughtful when they returned to the vehicles and looked back at the strangely sterile scene, picturing it when humanity transformed it into a vital thriving community.

But if the new landscape being carved out of the wilderness had caused them to pause and reflect, the first sight of the great Noyali dam astounded and overwhelmed.

The track had climbed steadily after leaving the settlement, occasionally bordering the new highway, and bringing a strange flash of incongruity each time the glare of concrete loomed alongside and was lost again in the wild green savannah. Then suddenly the car topped the rise and Venetia saw the entire construction site as though it were a vast scene set in a giant amphitheatre below.

The broad white highway snaked like a giant ribbon that drew the gaze to and over the great curve of the barrier dam. The sluice gates fell away beneath like stark rectangular teeth springing from the waste of churned earth and the mass of gaunt scaffolding. There was a sea of equipment, cement, skeletal shapes of girders, the rising geometric patterns of the hydro-electric plant, and the dwarfed figures of countless workers at the task which would not cease until the great project was complete. And beyond the man-made gash in the valley the hills drowsed under a soft haze of blue opaque mist.

Simon had leaned back and lit a cigarette while Venetia took in the awe-inspiring scene, and when at last she turned and gave a small wondering shake of her head he smiled.

'Vital statistics? It'll cost nearly a hundred and seventy millions by the time it's completed. The new lake will extend nearly ninety miles, irrigation will serve the whole of the northern province of Kawali, the hydro-electric capacity will reach two thousand and ninety megawatts, and the—'

'Simon!' she held up her hand. 'I can't take it in. It's too vast, too complex.' She looked back at the scene, her eyes full of the lights of wonder, and shook her head. 'Jason must be fantastically clever to see all this through.'

'Jason is. He's a genius.' Simon fell silent, his own eyes musing, as though he saw an oft-viewed picture from a new angle. He got out his cigarettes and as he lit Venetia's the green runabout drove into view along the new highway. Even from the considerable distance, Della and Johnny were distinguishable through the clear air. Simon said casually: 'How long have you known your friend?'

'Della? Oh, ages. We've shared a flat for nearly two years.'

'She's a bit older than you, isn't she?'

'Five years, but we get along fine.'

He nodded. 'You're very fond of her, aren't you?'

'Yes, because she's a very sincere and likeable person and so easy to get along with. I don't think I've ever heard anyone say— Oh, look!' She clutched at Simon's arm. 'They're driving along the top of the dam.'

Looking like a small green beetle, the runabout was now crawling along that slender white ribbon of road atop of the great curved sweep. Exactly halfway across it stopped and the two tiny figures alighted and walked to the parapet, to gaze down that vast white wall dropping into the valley hundreds of feet beneath.

Venetia caught her breath. 'Oh, come on, Simon,' she cried eagerly. 'How exciting to drive over it – like stepping into history.'

'No, not today.'

Hardly believing in his refusal, she gasped, 'But why not? It's safe enough, isn't it?' Her smile faltered. 'It – it's not going to collapse?'

'God forbid!' He shuddered. 'What a thought!'

'Then why can't we?'

'Because I doubt if your head for heights would survive the experience. That's why.' Abruptly he put the car into gear, turned it, and headed back down towards the others.

He was obviously unmoved by her patent disappointment, and she was silent most of the way to Lizard Rocks where they parked the car in a clearing and made their way along a twisting path among the strangely shaped masses of towering outcrop. After a few minutes' walk they heard the rushing tinkle of a streamlet musing through the still air and the famous rock came in sight.

'That's Lizard Rock,' Simon remarked, breaking the silence for the first time since they got out of the car.

She glanced up at the natural rock table on which the

elements had worn a curved sinuous shape that in silhouette was uncannily like that of an enormous sun-basking lizard, paused a second, then said, 'Yes,' in an unenthusiastic voice.

'And there's the waterfall.'

'It's a very pretty spot,' she said politely.

In actuality, it *was* a very pretty spot. She was standing in a wide glade, cool with lacy fern and shaded by the three enclosing sides of rock crop. From the clefts and crevices amid the rocks thin rivulets trickled and linked with one another to tumble with exuberant force into a deep pool overhung with a creeper curtain and fringed with rose red water blossom.

The rest of the party had already arrived. The older and more sedate members had sought shaded nooks to relax on rugs or groundsheets and two of the men were assembling the charcoal grill in readiness for the barbecue. Claire and Della had already changed into their swimwear and as Venetia and Simon approached Johnny appeared at the far side of the pool, scrambled agilely on to the rocks and took a header into the water.

'The changing place is through there.' Simon pointed towards a small, cavelike opening. 'But don't leave your clothes inside in case they collect insects.'

She looked doubtful for a moment, then without a word took her tote bag which he had been carrying and ducked into the little cave.

When she emerged, a little self-conscious in her brief two-piece in this pagan setting, Simon was already in the pool, floating lazily and exchanging badinage with the others.

She wandered to the edge, waved to the laughing Della, and hesitated a moment before she turned away and chose a spot to sit. Somehow the day was failing in its promise and she had an uncomfortable suspicion that the reason for that failing promise lay within herself. But how? And why? It was a perfect day. Intense blue sky, green shade and violet shadows to cloak the power of the incandescent gold of the African sun, a limpid pool and the tinkling plaintive murmurs of the cascade, friendly voices and carefree laughter . . .

'Can't you swim? Or are you just feeling lazy?'

She looked up into Jason's whimsical face and smiled. 'Just feeling lazy.' Her glance strayed across the pool, then averted from the dazzle and the glare from the white rocks at the far side. She said slowly, 'Jason, this won't be submerged when the dam opens or – or whatever it does?'

He shook his head and dropped to the grass at her side. 'It's the Nyuni Valley that is to disappear under the new lake. This section and Karimba won't be affected.'

She wrapped her arms round her knees, still aware of the slight sense of awe she always felt in Jason's presence, and wished she could express her admiration of his work. At last she said musingly: 'It's very wonderful. I've seen pictures of Aswan, but today is the first time I've seen a similar undertaking in actual reality.'

He smiled indulgently and patted her hand. 'I suppose it does look a little awe-inspiring at first sight. It's probably because you're concerned in the work of the unit at base here. It tends to give one a personal interest.'

He stayed there, chatting easily in his calm friendly way, and she began to realize how attractive Jason could be when he relaxed. It was not difficult to imagine the result if he chose deliberately to exert the mature assured charm he undoubtedly possessed, nor to imagine Claire experiencing a quite natural jealousy. But Claire was reputed to be a bitch, to lead him a dog's life. Was it true?

Certainly she betrayed little affection for him in public. But if you loved a person you showed it, tried to make them happy. If you didn't ... and they needed warmth and affection they looked elsewhere. Were Jason and Della ...?

She sighed deeply and tried to banish the worrying train of thought. Della was wise and also unselfish. She would never allow herself to indulge in an affair which could only bring unhappiness not only to herself but others. Jason's voice recalled her.

'If you're going to cool off you'd better do it now, young lady,' he said, getting to his feet and giving her a rock-strong hand to pull her to her feet. 'I think the chefs will be ringing the gong very soon.'

She was almost on the point of deciding that she wouldn't swim until later in the afternoon, then she saw Simon preparing to come out and an imp of perversity made her change her mind. As he pulled himself out she slipped into the water from a point at the opposite end.

Drew and Mac, with the supervisory assistance of Muriel Vanders, had prepared a lavish feast. Grilled steaks which had been kept cool in thermal freeze containers until required, small sweet potatoes in their jackets, eggplant and guava and fruit for every taste. The only mistake was a cheese, limp and semi-liquid, and of such overbearing odourness that it was offered as a sacrifice to the pool spirit ... 'No swimming in there for a week!' Johnny grinned.

And now the little party gave themselves up to ennui, retreating to the shade out of range of those lethal rays ... Only Venetia remained awake, almost hidden in the black shadows near the waterfall. The spray was cool, near enough to play on her outstretched arm, and for a long while she watched the flashing courtship of a pair of huge gauze-winged dragonflies. She was almost surrendering to drowsiness when a light touch ran down her spine.

She jumped and gave a gasp, and Simon said, 'Okay, that was strictly non-hostile.'

She dropped her face against her arms and gave a non-committal murmur. There was a moment of silence, then the slight rustles of his movements as he sat down. Presently he remarked casually: 'That shocking rash seems to have cleared up nicely.'

She gave another murmur and did not move.

'What's the matter?' His tone was light. 'Are you still sulking because I wouldn't drive you over the dam?'

'Of course not. Why should I?'

'How should I know?' he said equably.

How indeed? She blinked at a silvery fern an inch from her nose and wondered how this situation had come about. Honesty forced her to admit that there was a modicum of truth in Simon's unerring probe, but pride would not allow the humility of granting him the admission. She veered away from the instant suspicion of the derisive teasing that would undoubtedly result were she to do so, and while she pondered the urgent little desire to resolve this strained situation a shower of spray descended over her back and shoulders. She twisted up to meet his mocking grin and her temper snapped. Prevarication and pretence vanished and she cried sharply:

'That's why! Nobody's ever serious about anything here.'

'What? Can't you take a splash of water now?'

'No, it isn't that. I'm just fed-up with being treated as though I were a kid. Nobody ever tells Della she can't ride over the dam in case she hasn't a head for heights, or – or hauls her back if she steps out into the darkness, in case she stands on a snake, or talks to her as if she hadn't

118

enough sense to come in out of the rain! Well, I've had enough of – of being the little girl that isn't sophisticated enough to be bothered with!' The burst of indignation choked on a sob and she burrowed her face hard against her forearms.

There was a long silence, so still she knew he had not gone away, then the quiet voice said: 'Oh dear, I didn't realize you felt as inadequate as all that.'

'I'm not inadequate. It's just that some people seem to think I am.'

'Well, if you're not inadequate I suggest you turn over. I'm not inclined to start reasoning with the back of your head.'

'You needn't bother, thanks,' she said in a muffled voice.

'But I'm going to bother. And if you don't face up by the time I count three I'm going to throw you in the pool.'

'You wouldn't dare.'

'Wouldn't I?' A pause, then, 'One ... two ...'

The quiet purpose in the calm tone froze Venetia into instant tensity and the sudden conviction that he was quite capable of carrying out his threat. On the slightly menacing 'Three ...' she raised her head and then, as slowly as she dared, turned on her side and propped herself on one elbow.

The grim face regarding her betrayed no hint of suppressed humour, and defiance in her glare was somewhat lessened by the slight quaver of her 'Well?'

'That's better,' he said dryly. 'Reason is prevailing.'

'You mean sheer brute strength,' she reminded him.

His brows went up and the grimness quivered at the corners of his mouth. 'It *is* an advantage – about the only one we have left.'

Unexpectedly she was finding defiance very difficult to sustain. The proximity of him, lean and bronzed and powerful in swim trunks, his dark steel gaze unwaveringly direct, was rather overwhelming at such close range. She lowered her gaze. 'Well, it's enough, for me, anyway,' she sighed.

The fight had gone out of her now, and for a moment he was silent, then he put a bunched fist under her chin and gently prised it upwards. 'For a start, why don't you stop comparing yourself with Della, or anybody else, for that matter?'

'I don't!'

'I think you do, secretly.' His hand fell away. 'Listen, little one. There will always be certain mortals in this life who shine more brightly than others, and use that shine to achieve their own way, whether it's good for them or not.'

'You don't have to wrap it up gently,' she said in a small cold voice. 'I'm perfectly aware that Della will always outshine me – and men will fall over themselves to grant her every whim. Like driving her over the dam!' she interjected bitterly. 'I realized that a long time ago, but it doesn't make any difference to our friendship because she's a very sincere and kind person. And I *don't* envy her, in spite of what you say.'

'Your loyalty does you credit, but I didn't say, or mean, that you envy her. I'm not even talking about your friend, not specifically, nor am I going to stress another certain little incident I noticed earlier this morning. I'm trying to point out that there's a surface shine about some people that's immediately obvious. If you are still fogged about what I mean I suggest you cast your mind back to the day you arrived here and saw Johnny.'

'Yes, you don't have to spell it out,' she said flatly.

'But it doesn't necessarily indicate an ultimately more satisfying attraction under the surface, and the average person of any discernment realizes this. He also realizes that all those other outshone mortals are every bit as potentially attractive as their more magnetic fellows. Oh, yes, I'll admit that men gravitate to the goddesses of this world like moths to a candle, but it's the inshine girls they marry.'

'Oh.' She could think of nothing else to say to this somewhat surprising little homily.

'Besides,' he added coolly, 'discovery is always more intriguing. Or do you prefer your discoveries unwrapped?'

'I – I never thought of it that way.' Some of her humour was beginning to return and an imp got through to her curving mouth. 'Of course some people prefer to see first what they're getting.'

'True.' He stirred and reached out to snap off a pink star-petalled blossom that interwined profusely in the creeper by the cascade. He inspected it, perhaps for lurking insects, and held it towards her. When she did not immediately accept it his mouth pursed in an audacious grin and he tucked the blossom in the slender hollow at the vee of her bikini top. His glance openly challenged her to flaunt the pagan tribute, and after a hesitation her hand dropped despairingly to the ground.

'Are you still unconvinced?' he said softly. 'You're a very attractive little girl, and you're going to be a very attractive woman some day – when the right man awakens you and sets light to that dormant glow.'

A flirtatious breeze rustled through the creeper and carried a warm spray of moisture on its wings, then suddenly it stilled and even the soft rushing murmurs of the cascade muted their music as Simon bent to her lips.

She quivered, taut as a bowstring under his hands, then it was too late to evade the claim of his mouth. Yet the firm kiss held the element of restraint and when she suddenly struggled he drew back, but without releasing her.

'Well?' His eyes teased.

'S-someone might – see!'

'What if they do?' With deceptive skill he was making it very difficult for her to escape. 'Would it be so terrible if they did?'

'I – I—' She moved her head almost despairingly. The light caress that had strayed to the nape of her neck and tangled in her hair seemed to be affecting her power of speech and she dared not look at him. 'I – I suppose not,' she managed in the last second of respite before it was too late.

When at last Simon stayed the kiss she no longer remembered the possibility of an audience. Her entire being awakened, and the shattering realization that she didn't care if anyone did see! She stirred, and the little pink flower fell to the ground between herself and Simon, its waxen petals crushed and limp, and her instinctive reaction was to seize it and replace it, where it might hide the betraying hammerbeats of her heart.

He interpreted the checked gesture and with calm deliberation reached forward and completed its intention, then looked up at her with that dark, unreadable gaze.

Slowly he took her hands and drew her unresistingly to her feet. With no trace now of the passion of those recent overwhelming kisses he touched his lips lightly to her brow and said with an enigmatic smile: 'You're beginning to grow up at last, little one.'

CHAPTER SEVEN

THE day had fulfilled its promise after all, a radiant, enchanted fulfilment that not even a roaring earth-drowning torrent could quench.

The rain blinded, swamped, made everything imposs-ible except huddling in the meagre shelter of the rock crannies and waiting for it to cease. When at last the little party squelched back along the morass that had been the path it was to find the vehicles so waterlogged that baling out seemed the only apt remedy. Venetia's clothes clung to her soaked body, her hair looked as though she had just come out of the shower, and red mud was daubed liberally over the poplin slacks that were caked round her ankles. If it was any consolation the rest of the party were similarly affected, but she did not need the consolation, there wasn't an iota of space in the wondrous exultation that crammed her world.

She was oblivious of the discomfort of sitting in pools of moisture in the tourer, or of the actual steam that rose from her as the sun blazed down again and dried the mud to plaster round her ankles and her hair to stiff rats-tails on her brow. Heaven was the circle of a man's arm thrown carelessly round her shoulder as he drove with miraculous one-handed skill; paradise the memory of his kiss; Eden a magic glade wherein he had made her aware of desire and her womanhood ... oh, Simon! her heart sang, the name was a rhapsody ...

'Bath night! He skidded to a halt and grinned. 'And you need one!'

'Take a look in a mirror,' she returned pertly.

'Not likely. I'll be along in half an hour. Mind you don't keep me waiting.'

'I'll try not to.' She skipped out, was checked by his 'Hey!' and realized she'd forgotten her tote bag. He handed it over, gave a small salute that was part mocking, part tender, that made her heart turn over and increased the blitheness in her step as she danced into the bungalow. She had to bath and change – they were all adjourning to the Kinlays' for the rest of the evening – what should she wear for Simon? If only she had something new and fabulous to put on ... but first there was something very important she had to do ...

The pink blossom was crumpled and limp and sorry for itself, but she smoothed out the petals with tender fingers, found a piece of clear polythene and carefully sealed the pressed flower. Now for a book ... if only she had one of her old, well-loved ones here with her ...

'All clear in the bathroom, pet. Hallo, what have you got there?'

'Nothing.' Hastily she swept the book and its secret into a drawer and concealed it beneath a jumbled layer of undies. 'Is the water hot, Della? I'm caked. What are you wearing?' She was grabbing wildly at things, putting them down again. 'I'm sick of everything I brought! I say, what was it like looking over the edge of the dam? I'd have been absolutely petrified! Simon refused point-blank to let me go on it. We're going to have that fun week-end, by the way. In two weeks' time. He knows some people there and we're going to stay with them. Oh, bother! my scent's been running out all over my hankies. Della, can I borrow some of your talc and body lotion? That exotic French stuff?'

'Help yourself.' Della's expression was frankly interested. 'But hadn't you better switch off the generator first?'

'Generator?' Venetia almost came back to earth.

'Darling, if you don't switch off before you add my *Fabergé Aphrodisia* you'll go up in blue smoke.' Della smiled. 'It's a heavenly experience, isn't it?' Without elaborating on whether this referred to falling in love or going up in blue smoke she beckoned mysteriously and added, 'If you care to float into my room I have something which may fit the occasion.'

Venetia promptly obeyed, laughing at Della's hasty injunction to keep her muddy feet near the door, and watched the older girl reach into her wardrobe. When she turned she was holding a certain garment that brought a decidedly green glint into Venetia's bright eyes.

'You've always liked this, haven't you?'

'This' was a model Della had gone rash on a few weeks before her departure. It was of champagne-tinted very heavy lace, with a square neckline and sleeveless, and was so deceptively simple at first glance to make one gasp at the astronomical figure Della had paid for it, but when one got inside it and slinked before the mirror its sheer French chic drove more sordid considerations far enough . . .

'I'm afraid it's the most extravagant mistake I've ever made,' Della sighed. 'Somehow the colour makes me look just a trifle sallow, and now with this tan . . . But you're fairer-skinned.'

Venetia grappled with temptation, then shook her head. 'I'd adore to wear it, but this would be the one time somebody would tip a glass of something over me. Thanks for the thought, though.'

'You can have it,' said Della carelessly. 'You know it fits, and I've never worn it here, so it won't be recognized, but you might have to take it up if it's not short enough for you.'

'Mean it? Really?' Venetia swooped to hug her friend. 'I'll pay you back when we get home. Yes! I insist. But I haven't got much time. Got any thread that'll match?'

Della threw the dress on the bed and groaned. 'Go and wash. Go on, or I'll take it back. They're coming in twenty minutes.'

Giggling, Venetia fled, to take the quickest scrub on record. When she returned to the bedroom Della was halfway round the hem. She looked up. 'I'm only tacking it – you'll have to do it properly before you wear it again. Thank goodness it's lace – the stitches don't show. And don't stand there looking like love's young dream lost in space! Start dressing.'

'Yes, Della. I'll do the same for you one of these days.'

'You can do something now.' Della snapped the thread and thumb-pressed quickly along the fold. 'Go plug in the iron – and keep your eyes off Johnny tonight.'

'Who's Johnny?' Venetia asked innocently, trailing one stocking as she hopped to the door. 'Have I met him?'

By a miracle they were ready with two minutes to spare before their escorts arrived. 'But only because we were slightly delayed,' said Johnny, affecting a teasing, don't-believe-you air.

Venetia was suddenly overcome by silence when she came face to face again with Simon. Half an hour was such a short space of time, yet it seemed an age since they had parted after the return drive from Lizard Rock. Perhaps it was the darkness, or because Della and Johnny were present, or the long, considering glance that had travelled over the lace dress. He had inclined his head, as though in appraisal, but now, strolling along to the Kinlay home, she wondered what he thought . . . did he remember this afternoon? Did he remember . . .? Suddenly she was grateful for the darkness, for the discreet veil it cast over the warm colour she could feel deepening in her cheeks. Had she surrendered too quickly to his kiss . . . betrayed that surge of emotion he had invoked? Had he guessed at the momentous thing that had happened to her . . . did he know how crazily she had lost her heart into his keeping?

He was so silent she had to glance at him, as though to reassure herself that he was still there, and at the sight of the dark outline of him, casual as he walked with that long, relaxed stride of his, some of the wondrous buoyant elation ebbed a little. Had that kiss meant as much to him? He had given every indication of finding her attractive – he must have done, or he wouldn't have made love to her. But . . . Venetia stole another small glance and the first doubt came; maybe it hadn't meant anything at all to him, maybe one kiss had just led to another . . . some men made love to girls just for the sake of making love, without being in the least bit in love with them. But Simon wasn't that kind of a man; he wouldn't kiss a girl unless he – *liked* her a little. She sighed as they climbed the steps to the Kinlay verandah; she had had so little experience to be able to judge what a man might do, or what his motives might be when he did . . .

The slight sense of awkwardness persisted for quite a while that evening. Unconsciously she was waiting for Simon to make the next move, and completely unconscious of what form she expected that move to take. As was usual at Claire's do's, there was eating and drinking and nibbling and more drinking, interspiced with an inquest on the day's events. But it was not until Claire put on a record and suggested dancing that she experienced for the first time the sheer agony of physical jealousy. Simon took Claire in his arms, Johnny took Della, and it was Jason who drew Venetia into the wide cleared space in the big room.

He was a competent dancer and, more important, a pleasant, considerate partner, and at any other time she would have thoroughly enjoyed dancing with him. But she could not forget Simon, so near yet so remote from her, or prevent herself from trying to distinguish the murmurs of his voice intermingling with Claire's silvery tones.

At the finish Jason said, 'How nice to dance with a partner who doesn't chatter all the time.'

For a moment she thought it was a gibe at her pre-occupation, but his expression was quite sincere and his 'Save me another one,' effectively banished the suspicion.

'I like dancing without talking as well,' she said shyly, and then knew that Simon was coming across the room. *Was this all part of it? The senses that screamed their knowledge before sight and hearing registered the substantial?* It took a supreme effort of will not to turn, to slip into his arms before he opened them, but she succeeded in resisting that force until the tone arm of the record player swung with agonizing slowness into the run-in groove . . .

Strangely, she felt small, awkward in his arms, conscious of trying to foretell his steps. The music was hauntingly familiar, yet she could not place it, then she stumbled and gave a small impatient murmur. Why wasn't it the way she had expected? Why wasn't it an effortless drift into his arms, a supreme joy of convergence transcending the mere mechanics of moving?

Suddenly he said: 'That dress isn't you.'

'What?' Her head came up so sharply it almost bumped

128

his chin. 'What's the matter with it?'

'Nothing.' He smiled slightly. 'Except that it's the kind of dress that gives a misleading impression of the girl inside it.'

'Oh.' She looked at the small white shirt button that was exactly level with her eyes and wondered what response he might expect to that unexpected statement. A statement that became more disturbing the more she thought about it. 'I thought you were sufficiently perceptive to discern beyond outward appearances.'

Imperceptibly his hold tightened. 'I'm sorry, that was an ill-favoured observation. It's a very beautiful dress, little one.'

Instantly she forgave him, even when he murmured in exactly the same tone, 'But I haven't changed my opinion.'

The mocking tenderness imbued Venetia with rash courage and the impulse to provoke. Without pausing to consider whether she could emerge the victor in a contest of wiles with Simon Manville, she allowed herself to melt just a little more against him and said lightly: 'Supposing it isn't the dress that's giving the misleading impression. Would you revise your opinion then?'

There was a pause, then, 'I'm always prepared to admit I'm mistaken.'

The tone had given nothing away, and Venetia sought for a brilliant riposte that didn't seem to be forthcoming. The thought glimmered that she was fighting without a foil, and at the same moment he slowed his steps, bringing her almost to a standstill, and said in a forceful whisper: 'But not until the mistake is proved.'

His shoulders were effectively screening her from the room, and behind her the veranda window was within brushing distance of her dress. He released her hand and gestured towards the night outside. 'Would you care to discuss this difference in private?'

Venetia went tense, then ceded to defeat. The curve of that lean mouth and the sardonic hand still indicating the screen seemed to scream a silent warning that any discussion in private was liable to get out of hand – *her* hand! – and even though the mere thought was enough to start her spine trembling she managed a small smile of dissent and a shake of her head. 'But I'm not in the mood for intellectual exercise, Simon – only for dancing!' she added hastily, sensing another of the pitfalls that any unwary choice of statement could open before her feet when Simon was around.

His mouth twitched and he shrugged, saying nothing until he had drawn her back on to the floor. 'A pity,' he remarked with convincing regret, 'I was about to admit that I *had* made a mistake.'

'Really?' She would not look up. 'I don't believe you.'

'Oh, yes. A week or so ago I wouldn't have believed you were capable of wiles.'

'Well, now you know.' The elation of triumph crept into her tone.

He nodded. 'But it would be wiser in future to defer them until you've the courage to follow them through.'

Her breath stayed, waiting.

'Didn't you know, little one, that to melt into a man's arms is the most potent invitation of all?'

'Oh, did I?' she said in a small voice, dismay making her forget to prevaricate.

'You certainly did.'

The end of the record and someone announcing that they could do with a drink saved Venetia from having to fend off that one. She sat down weakly on the nearest chair and fanned her flushed face, aware that her breathlessness wasn't entirely due to dancing exertions. Nevertheless, the excitement within her was exhilarating and joyous. For the first time she was becoming aware of the dormant woman-power awaking within her, of the Eve responding to the challenge of an attractive man and seeking to test that power. She remembered something Simon had said that evening on the verandah when she'd been so desperately unhappy over Johnny's failure to notice her. She'd protested against his infuriating habit of calling her a little girl, and he'd said, *"But you are a little girl – as far as the man-woman correlation is concerned."* At the time she had believed she understood his meaning, that he implied that she was still young in years and naïve in her approach to the opposite sex. Now she was beginning to perceive how little she'd grasped of the complexity to which he had referred. Oh, yes, she now knew all about falling in love with him! And the potent, hitherto unsuspected ecstasy his touch alone could invoke. The presence of him could dwarf everything in the radius of him, an unexpected glimpse of him could make her heart contract, the sound of his voice subdue all other sounds . . . But there was a great deal more to it than that; had she the power ever to effect that transformation in Simon himself?

He was turning, to come back to her with their drinks, and she dragged her gaze away, suddenly afraid it betrayed the intensity of her thoughts, and met the long, considering stare of Claire.

As though it were by some prearranged signal, she drifted across the room. Della and Johnny moved at the same time, and they all converged into a small group as Simon came with the drinks.

He did not set hers down beside his own but held it out to her. Somehow her fingers fumbled as she accepted it and some of the liquid tipped over the rim of the tall glass. His reflexes were instant. He clamped one hand on the glass while his knee thrust Venetia's thigh aside. The rain of crystal drops missed her dress, and the pressure on her thigh eased. 'Got it now?'

She nodded, shaking her wet hand, and he straightened. Then she exclaimed: 'Oh, it's gone over you!'

Instinctively she reached forward to brush at the moisture beads on the dark immaculate material, and he shook his head, moving out of reach. 'Don't worry.'

She became aware of the silence, and the audience still intent on the tiny incident which had lasted only seconds. She looked away from Simon, forcing a natural smile and raising her brows at Della as though to say: *'See, what did I tell you?'* and Claire chose that moment to drop the bombshell that was to bring Venetia's happiness to ruin.

'By the way ...' Claire's wide blue gaze roved innocently between Simon and Johnny, 'who won that little wager between you two? And more important – who paid up?'

There was a blank silence. The two men stared and Jason frowned. Venetia's glass stayed poised in mid-air, not quite reaching her parted lips. Claire's eyes were direct on her face and they sent unease.

Claire smiled carelessly, affecting surprise. 'What's the matter? Have I said something frightfully *outré*? Surely it isn't still a secret? I mean,' she gestured, 'we can all see how it worked out.' Her glance clearly coupled Venetia and Simon, and Della and Johnny. 'Can't we, darling? Jason and I just wondered which of you two Lotharios won the fiver.'

Simon's face was like a mask. He might not have heard for all the expression it held, then Johnny grinned sheepishly behind his hand and said, 'Can't you guess?' His arm went round Della's shoulders. 'But she's worth it, even though she hasn't forgiven me yet.'

'I should say it was void, if not illegal under Kawali gaming laws,' said Jason lightly, 'but I'm prepared to play croupier and settle it. Claire, did you know we're practically *dry*?'

'Darling, we're not!' Her attention was diverted to Jason at the cocktail cabinet. 'I checked up only last Wednesday.'

'So I notice,' he surveyed the row of bottles sardonically, 'but you forgot the Pimms, and there's no lager or Export.'

She made a face. 'I don't drink beer, darling.'

'No, but we do.' Jason's voice was curt. He glanced round. 'Sorry, folks, you'll have to drown your sorrows the hard way until I pick up a fresh crate.'

Simon said, 'I'll go. I need some cigarettes. Got the keys handy, Mac?'

Jason made a mild protest while Mac produced the store keys and tossed them over. Simon caught them neatly. 'I need some air, anyway. Like to share it?' he added as he came abreast of Venetia.

For a long moment she stared at him. The pieces were falling into place, and fitting too well. It was all too painfully clear. Simon and Johnny had been amusing themselves. It had all been a joke . . . everyone knew, except . . . she swallowed hard. Any moment now disillusion was going to exact its inevitable toll and she was going to . . . Her mouth set, as though to repress the hot dry burning behind her eyeballs that craved tears to lave its sting. She met Simon's unsmiling glance.

'No, thanks,' she said coldly. 'I'm not staying much longer – it's late already and I – I want to – to wash my hair,' she ended wildly.

For a moment he looked down at her averted face, then walked out of the room.

She waited until the door swung to behind him, then scrabbled in her bag for a cigarette. Jason had followed Simon out, cupping his hands to the cigarette he was lighting, and with frozen calm Venetia stood up and made her way to escape, ignoring Claire's light aside: 'Is everybody leaving?'

But Jason was returning. He gave his friendly look, noted the cigarette she'd already forgotten, and observed: 'You're not lit. Here . . .' His lighter sparked into flame. Abruptly his eyes narrowed.

'You're trembling. Okay, Ven?'

She nodded emphatically. 'I'm fine.'

'You don't look it,' he said bluntly. 'Don't be ill again.'

Her mouth quivered. 'Please don't fuss, Jason,' she begged, silently imploring him to understand. 'I'm just tired and—'

'I'll see you back. Yes,' he took her arm, ignoring protests. 'Got your things?'

It was too much effort to argue. With the ease of the authority which was second nature to Jason, he closed the lounge door, isolating Venetia from the laughter now sounding from within, and piloted her out into the night. He didn't talk, and he gave no indication of noticing her strained miserable face or the control that would crack at the first unguarded word. However, when they reached the gate of the girls' bungalow, he solemnly put his hands on her shoulders and shook her gently.

'I know. It was distasteful and unfunny. And obviously you didn't know. But you mustn't take it to heart. Now cheer up. Do you hear?'

She sighed deeply and nodded.

'It's awfully bad for discipline, you know,' he said whimsically, 'and if it's any consolation to you I intend inflicting a damper of long overdue discipline on this unit. From tomorrow there'll be no time for any more heads-you-win, hearts-you-lose nonsense.' He paused, a flicker of doubt crossing his face. 'I'm not putting my foot in it, am I? There isn't some other cause for – this?' He eyed the woebegone young face. 'Because if you have any problems you must come to me. You're very young, too young. You make me aware of my responsibility every time I see you.'

'There's nothing wrong, Jason. Nothing.'

'Then cheer up. You won't believe me – but you won the right man. Or rather, the right man won you. Now off you go and forget about it.'

He patted her shoulder, murmured a good night, and waited until she had disappeared indoors.

But even though she was thankful it had only been Jason – at that particular moment she couldn't have taken plain speaking from anyone else – there wasn't a grain of comfort in those final unqualified statements. *The right man!*

The only bitter comfort she could derive was from the memory of passing Simon under the lantern at the Kinlay gate as he returned with the crate of lager and she was leaving – and hurrying past him as though he didn't exist.

*   *   *

'But, darling, be reasonable! They only did exactly as we did! They flipped a coin!'

'I don't feel reasonable.'

'Then try to be logical,' Della exclaimed impatiently. 'Heavens, they didn't know us then! They probably thought of it in the same light as we did. For a bit of fun, and being men there had to be a fiver at stake.'

'And they both wanted you.'

Della heaved a sigh. 'If you've got that idea into your head nothing *I* say will ever shift it. Oh, Ven, for goodness' sake snap out of it. It's so puerile!'

Della's lack of patience was the last straw. Venetia pushed aside her breakfast roll and got up blindly from the table. 'It's true, isn't it?'

'No, it isn't. Come on, we're both going to be late.'

At this fresh realization Venetia gave way. She stared desperately at the misted pearl radiance of the lake under the early morning sun and shook her head. 'I can't. I can't face Simon Manville. Not after . . . not knowing . . . Oh, how could he? And I – I thought he . . .' She bowed her head and dashed her knuckles across her eyes, hating her own weakness but helpless before it.

'You thought what?' Della jumped up, and now there was dismay as well as impatience in her voice. 'Ven, you haven't lost your head over Simon Manville?'

There was no reply, except for the drooping shoulders and the downbent head. 'Oh, no!' Della sighed. 'What a baby you are! I might have guessed this would happen if I hadn't been . . .' She sighed again and walked to the window, to join Venetia in a worried contemplation of the morning scene. 'I thought you were just putting it on these last few days, like the way you went on when you went pie-eyed over Johnny.' She opened the screen and wandered out on to the verandah, then turned. 'Listen, Ven, it's no use being serious about Manville, You'll be crying for the moon.'

'I want the moon,' Venetia said dully. 'I love him.'

'Nonsense!' Della sounded brisker than she felt. 'He took a bit of notice of you and kissed you when you thought everybody was asleep, and gave you a bit of his man of the world patter, in an avuncular way, and you fell for it.'

Oh, no! Venetia groaned inwardly. *No, it wasn't like that. He ... Simon didn't throw a line like that ... he ...* But even as she tried to convince herself her heart grew cold, receptive to the assurance, the knowledge of Della's insight.

'I'm not trying to hurt you, pet,' Della said more sympathetically, 'just trying to point out that Manville's a different proposition altogether from Johnny. You know where you are with Johnny, he's a bit of a rogue and he's a flirt, but he's honest about what he's looking for and there's no hard feelings if the girl won't play. But Manville.... For one thing he's older, for another thing he's the quiet subtle type, and believe me, you have to be smart to stay one move ahead with that kind, and he's experienced – too experienced for you, my pet.'

'What do you mean – experienced?' Venetia said in a low voice.

'Well, darling!' The older girl spread her hands, 'he hasn't got to thirty-four without learning a bit about women. Not with his share of what makes a man tick. I'll admit he's a sheer hunk of magnetism, and I should imagine he knows how to operate, but as for falling in love with him ...' Della glanced at her watch and moved abruptly indoors. 'I should have thought even you wouldn't have been naïve enough not to recognize it.'

Venetia stayed unmoving, hardly hearing her friend's light movements of last-minute preparations to depart for the morning's work. She was still standing there when Della came out again, fresh, cool and soignée, and said resignedly: 'Well, do I say you have a headache?'

'No,' she said sadly, 'just say I'll be late – and if they sack me I don't care.'

'Don't be childish,' said Della sharply. 'Unless, of course, you *want* to make it obvious.'

Plain truths are always the most unpalatable, as Venetia was learning. During the days that followed she also learned the bitter feminine art of donning the mask of indifference. She still did not want to believe in Della's cool logical assessment of Simon's character. He wasn't all those things Della had said, that added up to dangerous attraction and experience. Of course he would be experienced, he wouldn't be mature otherwise, she reasoned, but that didn't make him untrustworthy or callous. *But you trusted him, and look what happened*, the cool little voice of sense reminded her. All those signs of ironic tenderness, the teasing, the safe bulwark he had been against the fears and wretchedness of that never-to-be-forgotten night that seemed so long ago, and the culmination of the day by the pool. Had it been the clamour of her own awakening senses that had fooled her into believing she was evoking the first tender response of affection in him?

But it had all been a joke. For a flip of a coin and a fiver. And how easily she had been beguiled! Resolutely she tried to close her heart against him. Never again would she trust him and allow herself to be gulled into unwariness.

It was fortunate that Jason did not forget his threat about discipline, and that the time had come for the transfer of the first group of Oskiri villagers into their new homes. This task, and the endless problems, large and small, it entailed, effectively removed Simon from base. His days were fully occupied at the settlement area and by the time he returned long after nightfall Venetia had completed her routine work and adjourned where there wasn't so much likelihood of encountering him. It was over a week before Della said suddenly:

'Where *do* you hide yourself at nights now?'

'At Muriel's. She's moving into her new quarters next week and there's masses to do. The clinic isn't opening officially until next week, but she wants to get all her stuff packed and ready, and then there's all the files and things to do. We're going over tomorrow, all day, to start registering the patients. She said I could help if it was okay with Jason. I'm looking forward to it.'

'Mind you don't bump into Simon.'

Venetia shrugged. 'It doesn't matter. There'll be so many people about and he'll be too busy, anyway.'

'Busy!' Della raised expressive brows. 'Jason's being an absolute slave-driver. I've to go along with him to the site tomorrow – the third time this week. And the little office he uses up there . . . it's like a steam bath. I don't know which is the worst, sitting in it and turning into a grease spot or following him around with my notebook at the ready and all those wolves whistling. Oh, well . . .' Della reached for her cleansing tissues, 'enjoy yourself at the health ministry.'

It proved a fascinating day, despite Della's wry bidding. As Muriel had said; there was a great deal to be done. The whole new township was a hive of movement and activities. Children milled everywhere, mixed with dogs and chickens and goats and the assortment of four and two-wheeled vehicles that streamed along the hot new road from the outlying countryside. Already the villagers were engaged in making the place look like home. The ragtag and bobtail of stalls were being set up in the narrow road between the clinic and the new school, and within a very short space of time tradition was going to camouflage steel and concrete and glass.

Muriel glanced across the surge of colour and sighed. 'What can you do? There's that huge area in the western sector that has been designated as the market place and they've ignored it, choosing this. We'll never get them to move now.' Her stern features had softened, and Venetia knew suddenly how much Muriel loved these people and the work she had chosen.

At first the mothers had been reluctant and suspicious to enter the streamlined white portal of the clinic, then persuasion and curiosity had prevailed. Now, the spacious reception hall was like bedlam as the children scampered and shouted after a thin dog with a long lank tail and a foolish face that had somehow gained admission. The mothers clustered in groups, most of them carrying toddlers in their arms, and all of them looking slightly bewildered. Some of them had dressed in their most colourful finery for the occasion, even though it was only to have their names registered by Noni and the lustrous-eyed Bantu girl who was assisting, and some of them were openly disappointed that no treatment was to be forthcoming at this stage.

'I think we might start weighing the babies,' Muriel said in an aside. 'It might ease the inital rush on the first few days and get them used to the idea.'

So Venetia stood by the scales, carefully noting the details down on the cards which she would later file in their appropriate places in records.

The hours flew past. Inevitably organization was broken down by the reality of circumstance. An old woman hobbled in and pointed mutely to an enormous ulcer on her leg. A child was brought in with a suppurating foot in which a thorn had long since lodged and the foot liberally plastered with an evil-smelling ointment that looked and smelled suspiciously like cow-dung. Dr. Vanders discovered three cases of impetigo, a woman with the grossly swollen limbs and 'leopard skin' characteristic of filariasis, and a child whose eyes were scarred with trachoma.

'Well, has this been enough to put you off the thought of nursing?' asked Muriel dryly when they eventually found time to sit down and snatch a cup of tea.

'No, I'll admit I felt a bit squeamish when I saw that woman's leg,' said Venetia, 'then I forgot about myself and just felt I wanted to help.'

'Yes, it gets you that way.' Muriel sighed, her eyes thoughtful. 'But I wouldn't advise you to get carried away with the idea.'

'I could train, though, couldn't I?' Venetia asked.

'Oh, yes, but not here, my girl.' Muriel smiled. 'You'd just begin to be useful, then you'd get married.' She shook her head at the instant denial forthcoming and smiled again. 'Take it from me, you'll be married before you're twenty.'

'How do you know?'

'I've seen too many young hopefuls, particularly in tropical nursing. They start off with the utmost sincerity – dedication, in fact, and please don't think I'm decrying their hopes, I'm not – and then along comes a man.' Muriel snapped her fingers. 'In the tropics the male-female ratio is too ill-balanced for it to happen otherwise. I remember one youngster at—'

'Dr Vanders ...' Noni stood at the door. 'You are wanted on the telephone. It's urgent. There has been an accident at the construction site.'

An accident! Venetia went icy with fear and dreadful premonition. *Simon*! But she'd glimpsed him twice during the course of the day. Once down near the temporary reception office set up to signpost the influx into the new township. He had been in conversation with two of the officials from Mortonstown and the chief of the Oskiri village which was at present in course of transference. The second glimpse had also been from a distance, as he was driving off somewhere. Now she thought of it, he had been heading towards the construction site.

Clammy with the cold sweat of dread, she waited for Dr. Vanders to come from the phone, and the brief spell of time seemed like a century as she feverishly imagined what might be. Noni had sounded frightened, as though shock and urgency had been conveyed from the message she had taken. Was it a disaster, men maimed, or worse? *Was it Simon?*

But it was not Simon. It was Jason.

CHAPTER EIGHT

'It was dreadful! I never want to live through anything like that again as long as I live.'

Della moved convulsively and finished the very stiff drink she had poured for herself. She looked into the empty glass and grimaced as she set it down. 'Thank God he's going to be all right.'

Venetia watched her anxiously. She had never seen Della so distraught, or her lovely face so haggard. Sensing that Della desperately needed the release of telling of it all, she said tremulously, 'What exactly happened? The rumours started flying within a few minutes of Dr. Vanders leaving the settlement.'

'We were just preparing to leave, I was in the car,' said Della, 'then Jason remembered something he wanted to check. He told me to wait. The shift had just changed, and masses of men were going off. Dozens of them come to work on bicycles, and I thought I'd just pull the car a bit further into the side of the track. You know how Citroens settle when you stop – something to do with the suspension – and somehow it felt different from the driving seat. I giggled a bit, and checked I'd put the brake on properly and it was then I noticed men running, and two boys on bikes nearly ran into me because they were pointing at something right across the site and shouting.'

Della took a deep breath. 'It was one of those great mechanical grab things. They must have been clearing debris. It started to tip and the grab thing was swaying on its chain, and then suddenly it toppled over.'

'Oh, no!' Venetia gasped.

'It seemed to fall so slowly, and the grab thing opened and what looked like a shower of earth flew all over. But there were rocks and all sorts of stuff in it, and Jason got hit. It knocked him flying. Oh, Ven, he's got the most ghastly shoulder, all gashed, and Muriel said he'd broken a bone in his arm in the fall.'

Della reached for another cigarette and lit it, her hand visibly trembling. 'I can't remember getting there, but I must have run all the way across. Jason was conscious, trying to get on his feet, but you could tell he was in dreadful pain. We got him to the first aid place and somebody phoned for Muriel, and we did what we could. Of course as soon as Muriel got there she went off the deep end because we hadn't rushed him straight to hospital. But he had refused to hear of it when somebody suggested it, you know what Jason's like. Anyway, Muriel gave him an injection and carted him straight off to Mortonstown. I followed along in the car in case there was anything else I could do, and somebody sent for Claire.' Della gave a shuddering sigh. 'The wretched woman went and had hysterics, all over the bed, and Simon Manville, saying she wanted to get Jason home and get a specialist. God! It mightn't be Barts, but the hospital seemed to be a bright enough, modern place.'

Venetia got up restlessly. 'I hope he'll be all right. Did they say anything?'

'Oh, the usual. He was comfortable. I saw him for a few moments before I left and he was quite lucid. They'd X-rayed his arm and shoulder and set the arm, and Claire started moaning that she'd heard somewhere that plaster could cause ulcers in the tropics. I could have throttled her! Anyway, Simon took her away to some friends. He's going to stay there, for tonight, anyway, and I brought the car back. That was another nightmare. I kept seeing Jason and . . .' Della shuddered and slumped wearily back. '*Why* did it have to be him?'

'I don't know. Thank heaven it wasn't worse.' Venetia stood by Della's chair and looked down worriedly at her. 'Come on, Del. It's nearly two in the morning. Go to bed and I'll fix you something light. You must be absolutely bushed.'

With some urging, she persuaded Della to go to bed and eat one of the thin sandwiches she had made. But it was obvious that Della would not sleep easily. Looking at her strained face, the dark hair for once tumbled and untidy, she sighed for the calamity which had overtaken Jason. What was going to happen next?

The accident cast a cloud over the entire project and the personnel. Della hovered by the phone practically all the following day, and even Johnny's efforts to cheer her had no effect. At about ten o'clock Simon rang to say that Jason was quite comfortable and had left instructions that everyone was to continue routine work as best they could until he got back.

Venetia looked at the phone Johnny had just put down and felt the surge of longing swamp over her. It seemed so long since she had heard Simon's voice, touched him, looked at the quirks of that mobile mouth as it curved in the mocking tender smile that made her heart lurch. But it was too late to regret the bitterness that had made her deliberately avoid him, and assume a cold unfriendly attitude on the few occasions she had come into contact with him. The misfortune that had befallen Jason had put the affair of the wager into true perspective, shown it for the triteness it really was, but it was still too late. And nothing was changed, nothing that mattered as far as Simon was concerned. She'd fooled herself all along. If she had mattered in even the tiniest way to him he

145

could have found some way of seeking her out. But he hadn't bothered. Therefore she didn't matter to him and the sooner she resigned herself to that obvious fact the sooner her bruised heart might cease to ache. If it ever would . . .

Two days later Jason discharged himself from hospital.

On the Tuesday evening, quite late, he sent instructions that Della was to use his car and be at the hospital as early as she could make it on the Wednesday morning.

The transformation in Della was instant. She looked as though she were suddenly relieved of a tremendous burden. Assuming that Jason was now feeling sufficiently recovered to take on as much control as was possible from a sick bed, she set off at dawn, taking with her the small battery tape recorder and everything else she could think of that he might require. When she arrived at the hospital it was to find a grim, indomitable Jason fully dressed and a worried, deeply disapproving doctor.

'Now don't *you* start,' was all he said before her shocked concern could be put into words, and so Della drove her very special passenger with the utmost care back to the base.

What a responsibility! Venetia thought, when she got over her surprise at the sight of Della returning so soon and the shock of seeing the reason. Jason looked dreadfully drawn and unsteady as he walked slowly into the office. One sleeve of his shirt hung empty, the band of a sling showed under the collar, and the white gauze dressing showed under the sticking plaster across one temple. However, he smiled faintly at the horrified expression Venetia could not disguise and said wryly: 'It's okay – I'm not quite such a wreck as I look.'

'Oh, no . . .!' she collected her wits and rushed to draw out a chair for him. 'Would you like a cup of coffee or something? I'll go and make some.'

'I'd like the something – with very little soda,' he said dryly as he sank awkwardly into his chair.

But Della was already splashing soda into a glass of whisky. Over her shoulder she said: 'Ven, are you not at the clinic today?'

'No,' Venetia looked uneasily at Jason, 'I thought I'd better stay here today. The place seems so deserted all of a sudden.'

'Because we're progressing towards the end – at last,' Jason said. 'Eventually this base will become merely a residential suburb for the technicians who take over when we all leave.'

Della was waiting until he had finished speaking. She said briskly, 'You'd better stay here for the present. You'll have to look after my work at this end until we get organized. I suppose you want to get along to the site as soon as possible,' she said to Jason.

'This morning, as soon as I've cleared up one or two things here. Any post?'

'Yes, here.' Venetia scurried. 'And Drew left these specifications last night for you to check, but he said they weren't terribly urgent.'

'Everything's urgent.' Jason finished the whisky and winced with an unguarded movement. 'And to start with,' he said irritably, 'could you do something about *this*? They've strapped me like a trussed chicken.' He seized the loose sleeve of his shirt and glared at it. 'If one of you could hack it off and I'd at least have the use of another hand.'

'All right, Jason,' Della said soothingly, and took a pair of scissors from the drawer of her desk. Calmly she sheared the sleeve away at the shoulder, leaving a large open arm-hole, then eased the garment off altogether. Very gently she undid the sling, supported the bound arm and motioned to Venetia to slip the shirt armhole over it. With remarkably little fuss his free arm was manoeuvred into the garment, Della buttoned it for him and then replaced the sling.

'There, all done by kindness,' she said with a note of affection.

'Thanks.' Jason flexed the fingers of the freed hand and wriggled it further out of the sling. 'You wouldn't think I had a devoted wife,' he said sourly. 'Now where's that specification?'

'Here.' Della laid the papers before him. 'Ven, you'd better rustle up that coffee. Then find one of the boys and send him up to Jason's house. What time do you want lunch, Jason?'

'I don't,' he said briefly. 'I'll have something on a tray in here.'

Della nodded to Venetia, her glance saying plainly: don't argue, and Venetia turned away, to halt at the door. 'Claire's here,' she said.

The tourer door slammed with a metallic thud and Claire hurried into the building, her silvery hair streaming in a cloud round her rose-clad shoulders. Behind her, Simon strode, his expression dark with anxiety. He passed Venetia as though he did not notice her standing there and came to a standstill as he saw Jason sitting at the desk.

'For God's sake, man!' he exclaimed above Claire's cry. 'What the hell are you doing here?'

'Working – I'm not dead yet.' Jason bent over the papers after the briefest acknowledgement of his wife's horrified gasp. He ticked the top page and passed it to Della. 'That's okay.'

'Jason!' Claire regained speech. 'You're not working! You can't.' She rushed forward. 'You should be in hospital. Why did you walk out? You—'

'Don't fuss.' Jason brushed her protests aside. 'Della, I need another drink.'

'Fuss!' Claire bent and swept the papers aside. 'I think you're out of your mind, Jason. You—'

Jason's hand thudded on the papers and his mouth set ominously. 'Leave me alone.'

'Claire's right,' Simon said quietly. 'You shouldn't be here.'

'And how did you get here? I couldn't believe it when they told me this morning.' She swung round to face Della. '*You* were responsible. How dare you take it on yourself to bring him back? Why didn't you tell me first? Sneaking around behind my back! What right have you to ignore the doctors, and me? If anything happens through this I'll hold you responsible. You—'

'Claire! Control yourself!' Jason snapped. 'She merely carried out my orders.'

'Oh, yes!' cried Claire furiously, open antagonism blatant now in the glare she turned on Della. 'I know all about your orders. The perfect secretary – *personal assistant*,' she sneered – 'but I'm not blind. And if you think I'm going to stand back and be spoken to like this! While *she*—'

'For Christ's sake, shut up!' Jason was on his feet, a flare of rage livid round his mouth. 'Now get out, the lot of you! Go on! Or I will!'

'Oh!' Claire took an incredulous step back. Her eyes widened unbelievably and her hand fluttered out. 'Jason, you're—'

'*For the last time* . . .' he gritted.

Still Claire stared at the dark angry features of the man behind the desk, then with a small sobbing cry she stumbled to Simon Manville. 'Please . . .' she said piteously, 'do something, Simon.'

For a long moment he looked at the implacable Jason, then with a curiously chilling glance at the white-faced Della he gave a slight shake of his head and touched Claire's shoulder. 'Not now.'

His own expression grim now, Simon led her out of the building. The slam of the car doors and the roar of the engine sounded unnaturally loud in the silence and broke the taut grip of anger that shimmered in the sunlit room. Jason sank back into his chair, winced and clasped his bound shoulder, and Venetia was jerked out of her frozen trance as she saw the ominous crimson stain.

Claire and the ugly little scene faded before this fresh disaster. She took a frightened step forward and faltered: 'Jason, your shoulder – it's bleeding.'

'Yes . . .' The word came on a long expelled breath and he dropped his head on his hand. 'One of the stitches has gone. Oh, the bitch! The damn, interfering bitch!'

Della straightened weary shoulders and reached for the phone. 'I'll get Dr. Vanders.'

*   *   *

'You're a fool, Jason,' Muriel Vanders said bluntly. 'Why you high-powered executives have to play God is beyond my comprehension. The whole truth of the matter is that you're so damned frightened in case somebody proves you're not indispensable, after all.'

'Yeah?' said Jason ironically, and gave a sudden groan, static under Dr. Vanders's firm deft hands. 'And don't put all that strapping back on, woman.'

'Like to call in a second opinion?'

'No, thanks. As I was saying – in a couple of weeks' time *you'll* be slogging away for twenty-five hours out of the twenty-four. Indispensable dedication.'

'That's different.' Muriel clipped off the end of the

bandage. 'Doctors expect to put their work before anything else. But I won't have a fractured ulna and six clips over the scapula region.'

'I could have said that last week.' Jason sat up cautiously and nodded. 'It feels a damned sight more comfortable than the strait-jacket they put on over there.'

'It won't stay very comfortable for long, not if you persist in racketing around as if you just had a cold in the head,' Muriel told him brusquely. 'You *should* be in hospital, for at least another week.'

Jason gave her an expressive look and leaned forward, glancing round the dispensary in search of his shirt. Muriel promptly placed a large hand on his uninjured shoulder and shook her head. 'You'll stay here for an hour until I'm certain the bleeding's stopped.'

A silent spectator, Venetia held her breath, fully expecting an outburst from Jason. But he didn't, merely relaxing back with a weary sigh of resignation. Certainly no one else would dare address him in the tone of voice Muriel was using, she reflected, still a little aghast at seeing a facet of Jason not previously glimpsed. He certainly packed a temper, and probably, in exclusively male company, a choice turn of language as well! And Claire . . . admittedly she was a flibberty-gibbet at times, but his treatment of her had been ruthless. She'd dissolved into tears, quite openly, when Simon had taken her away. Well, she'd never made any secret of having a yen for Simon and he seemed to reciprocate, Venetia thought bitterly, so doubtless she'd be enjoying a spot of consolation and Simon would be quite happy supplying it!

'Mind if we eat here?' Jason was asking sarcastically.

'Not at all. I'll join you.'

'To make sure I'm nailed for an hour.'

'You should have more sense than to need nailing.'

Muriel smiled blandly, and swept out of the room.

The moment she was gone Jason got up and retrieved his shirt. He looked at it with distaste and flung it down. 'Seeing that I'm incarcerated here for the next hour, who's going to volunteer to collect a clean shirt for me?'

Della stood up immediately, and Venetia said quickly: 'I will.'

'How nice to have such willing slaves,' Muriel observed as she re-entered.

'I treat them well.' Jason turned. 'While you're busy, Ven, will you bring some papers as well? They're in a buff folder with an A/7/JK reference on the front. They're among a pile of stuff under the map. Claire will give you them, if she's come to her senses by now,' he added grimly.

Had she? Venetia wondered as she walked down to the Kinlay house, thankful she had been there and saved Della the risk of facing an angry, vituperative Claire. Her steps slowed as she neared the gate and looked apprehensively across the garden. There was no one to be seen, the screens were all tightly closed against the midday heat, and the shadows beneath the veranda awning were a knife-edged black against the brilliant glare of the sun.

The heels of her sandals seemed unusually hollow as they clicked on the steps, and she was conscious of a slightly sick feeling at the pit of her stomach. Was Claire at home? Would she make a scene? But why should she? Her quarrel isn't with me, Venetia decided.

The door gave silently to her touch and swung inwardly. Tapping a couple of times, Venetia called, waited, and then gave an audible sigh of relief as she heard steps from the rear of the house.

'Claire, it's just me. I—' Her voice faltered into silence as Tomanje, the Kinlays' houseboy, appeared. He looked at her blankly, almost as though he were scared, and she said: 'Where's Mrs. Kinlay, Tomanje? Isn't she here?'

He shook his dark head and began to gesture. 'Missus not here. Missus gone.'

'Gone?' she echoed. 'Where?'

He waved his hands again. 'Don't know, Missy Ven.'

'But didn't she say?'

'No. She take things. Say she leaving. Say Mister Kinlay know all about it soon. She—'

The sick feeling was settling into a leaden weight of foreboding. 'What did she take, Tomanje? Was it luggage? Cases?'

He was going towards Claire's room, gesticulating and pointing to the open door, and one glance inside told Venetia that this was no casual trip. The wardrobe doors yawned wide, a drawer was half closed, oddments of clothes and tissue paper littered the bed and floor, and it was quite obvious that Claire had packed a great many of her personal things, and she had also packed in a wild angry hurry.

For a moment Venetia could not think straight, then she remembered the vital matter of transport. The Citroen was still parked outside the dispensary, exactly where Della had left it. How . . . ?

'How did she leave, Tomanje?' she demanded. 'Which car did she take?'

'The Bwana's, missy. He take her away. The Bwana Manville!'

*   *   *

Jason took the news with a stoical calm that was almost callous. After the miserable lunch with Muriel he departed for the construction site, Della driving, and Venetia was left to worry and wonder.

Johnny rolled back at sundown, heard the news, and

shrugged with a lack of concern that seemed little short of Jason's own reaction. 'Anyway,' he pinched Venetia's chin, 'what are you worrying for? You've no reason to weep for our errant Claire, or Jason for that matter. Or have you?'

'Oh, Johnny, of course not,' she sighed, 'but it's just so – oh, I don't know.' She shook her head hopelessly.

'It'll blow over. Come on, I'll take you for a drive down by the lake.'

A couple of months ago this invitation would have sent Venetia soaring into happiness. Now it merely brought a sad little smile to her lips and a refusal.

'I'm an expert at chasing blues,' Johnny said persuasively. 'Come on, try being sorry for me. I've lost my girl tonight.'

'She'll be back any minute now. It's dark.'

'Yes?' Johnny raised knowing brows. 'I guess she'll be fully occupied just the same.'

This had occurred to Venetia and her face clouded. With Claire gone and Jason in his present mood anything might happen. And how could anybody, even the hardest-hearted person, which Della definitely was not, refuse to take pity on Jason when he was injured and in pain, when only his toughness and willpower were keeping him on his feet? There could be little doubt as to whether Della would fail him, but at what cost? Venetia sighed again; how was it all going to end?

Johnny was shuffling his feet impatiently. He said suddenly: 'If you're missing Simon you're wasting your time, you know.'

'Am I? Who says I'm missing him?'

'I do,' Johnny teased.

'I hardly ever see him these days,' she returned coldly. Johnny shrugged. 'Well, he won't be back tonight, so you might as well take pity on me.'

While she still hesitated the glaring probes of the Citroen's headlamps stabbed into the night. It slowed slightly and slid to a halt outside the Kinlay bungalow. Venetia watched the white pools of light abruptly dissolve, heard the mingled voices as Della and Jason got out, and, after the finality of the silence when the voices were cut off by a closing door, turned to Johnny.

'No, I can't. I've got to talk to Della.'

But it was some time before Della's steps sounded slowly across the verandah and she came in, to collapse wearily in a chair.

'God, what a day!' She passed her hand over her brows. 'Fix me a drink, Ven, there's a pet.'

'Don't you think you're fixing too many drinks these days?' Nevertheless she went to obey. Della looked so desperately strained.

When she took the glass to her the older girl looked up and managed a wry smile. 'You're not going to start preaching at me, are you? I've had enough for one day.'

'You shouldn't have gone back with Jason tonight and stayed so long. Not after what's happened.'

Della shrugged. 'What else could I do? Somebody had to help the man. Have you ever tried doing all the ordinary everyday actions with one hand? If you haven't I suggest you try using your imagination, Ven.'

There was a flat note in her voice and a tautness round her mouth which Venetia had rarely seen before. She said more gently, 'The boy could have looked after Jason, surely.'

'Tomanje was missing. He probably thought nobody was going back there today and scarpered. It was less bother to fix things myself than go and root him out. Anyway, I had to talk to Jason.'

'You had all the afternoon to talk to him.'

'Yes – except that Jason has a one-track mind where his work's concerned. You know what the site's like, apart from the din, and trying to drive around without shattering Jason's serves as well as my own was enough for me without . . .' She tailed off to finish the drink and light a cigarette, then added:

'Anyway, your big heartache landed back half an hour ago.'

'Simon? Did he . . .?'

'He was empty-handed, if that's what you mean,' said Della dryly, 'and not showing a very sweet disposition.'

'So Claire didn't – change her mind.' Suddenly Venetia understood for the first time in her life that a drink could have a certain therapeutic effect at a time like this. She mixed herself a modest Martini and wandered aimlessly across the room. At last she said in a small worried voice: 'What's going to happen, Della?'

'How the hell should I know?' said Della irritably.

'You should.' Venetia swung round. 'It must be obvious that Claire thinks you're having an affair with Jason. The worst of it is, I think it's my fault.'

'Yours?' Della was shaken out of her weary apathy. 'How on earth has it anything to do with you?'

'No, you see I overheard Claire one night when she was talking to Simon, it was several weeks ago . . .' Venetia took a deep breath and recounted the conversation on which she had unwittingly eavesdropped. 'I was going to tell you, then somehow I couldn't. Now I wish I had. If only I'd warned you . . .' she finished sadly.

Della was silent for a little while, then she shrugged. 'I doubt if it would have made much difference, the way things are.'

'What do you mean?' Venetia felt cold. 'Della, *are*

you having an affair with Jason?'

'Not quite.'

'What do you mean? Not quite?'

'Darling,' a trace of cynicism came through in Della's smile, 'you surely don't believe I spent this evening seizing the opportunity to seduce another woman's husband, do you? Even you, my naïve pet, must realize that a man with a crocked shoulder and a fractured arm is labouring under a slight handicap. Even though your arrogant Mr. Manville looked down his nose and obviously thought the worst.'

Della paused and ran her hand through her hair, and now her smile was rueful. 'Believe it or not, but I spent the best part of an hour tonight trying to persuade Jason of the fact that his wife undoubtedly loves him, and that if he expounded a little more of his affection on her and less on steel and blueprints she'd be a lot happier and so would we all. Oh, we know Claire's a spoilt butterfly, but she's bitchy and unhappy because she loves him. I'd be as jealous as hell if I were Claire.'

'And what about Jason?' Venetia asked slowly.

'He's had enough.' Della sighed deeply. 'I always suspected Jason was as hard as granite under that whimsical urbanity of his and tonight I knew I hadn't been mistaken. Jason wants to have his cake and eat it.'

Venetia moved restlessly and took the two glasses back to the tray. 'You still haven't answered my question. Where do you fit in?'

For a long while Della did not reply. Then she got to her feet and flung an empty cigarette packet into the waste-paper basket. 'I don't know – yet.'

'You mean, you *are* involved?' Venetia said with dismay. 'Oh, Della, I always thought you ... Oh, I don't know,' she sighed helplessly.

'I wish I did,' Della said slowly. 'I enjoy my relationship with Jason. I enjoy the sense of being an invaluable third hand, the camaraderie of working in partnership with him. I couldn't bear to work with another woman. It would drive me crazy. I don't want to leave Jason and the most satisfying job I've ever had, just because a jealous woman thinks I'm trying to oust her.'

'Aren't you?'

'No, not deliberately.'

'It's still the same thing, whether it's deliberate or not,' Venetia said quietly. 'The thing is, are you in love with him?'

'Oh, God!' Della closed her eyes. 'Do you think I'd be agonizing here if I didn't? *Yes!* Yes, I love Jason. And how I wish I didn't.'

'So it's true, after all,' Venetia said sadly.

'It isn't as easy as that. It might be – if Jason felt the same way.'

'And doesn't he?'

Della shook her head. Frowning, she lit another cigarette and flung herself into a chair. 'You can't have cut-and-dried relationships like that, take one apart and isolate it. Oh, I'll admit there've been one or two incidents. Jason can be pretty controlled at most times, but control works two ways – when it goes it can be disastrous, and Jason's no exception. Why do you think I went off with Johnny? I never had the slightest intention of being involved with Johnny, but I'd no other choice.'

'So it *was* all a blind. Claire wasn't being fanciful and spiteful.'

'Yes, it was a blind. But it wasn't for her benefit. It was for Jason's. It was the only way I could convince him I had no intention of getting involved in an affair that would ruin everything. But it didn't succeed. God! I wish

I'd never come out here.'

Strangely enough, Venetia believed her. She said slowly, 'If Jason were free would you marry him?'

'I don't know. I honestly don't know,' Della said wretchedly.

'But if you love him . . .'

'For Jason I doubt if it would be enough. Oh, I don't know if I can explain so that you'd understand. I don't think any one woman could combine the qualities to make Jason completely happy and satisfy the demands of a near-genius.'

With a sudden perception Venetia began to compreend what Della was trying to put into words. Jason needed Della almost as much as he needed his wife. He needed those qualities of understanding Della possessed in abundance, the ability to share his working and routine problems and foretell what he was going to ask for almost before he knew himself. Della possessed the highest degree of perfection required in a career-man's assistant; she was clever, she was unflappable, she possessed acute perception and understanding – but she was also beautiful. The outcome was inevitable, sooner or later.

'You see,' Della mused, 'if I ever marry I should want to make my marriage as perfect and successful as I made my career. I should want my husband to put me and our children on an equal par with his work, and not bring his work constantly into our home life. Jason shouldn't have married anyone. He isn't a family man. If he'd given Claire a child things might have been different. He might have become different, who can tell? Jason is a lot of things. He's strong, generous materially, he has a way with people that makes them willing to slave for him. I would be fooling myself if I didn't admit I'd been his most willing slave of all. But I can love him and still recognize one unpalatable fact: basically Jason's selfish. I've accepted that. I'm paid to accept it. But will Claire ever accept it?'

From some unsuspected crevice a huge amber-winged moth emerged. Its wings whirred madly, and their beating against the lamp shade made a strange velvety rhythm in the silence after Della stopped speaking. Venetia watched the vibrating shadow of the insect and made an abortive attempt to waft it out of the room. But the insect homed back unerringly for the radiance and sighing she switched off the light, waiting until those soft frantic whirrs ceased.

Della stirred and blundered across the shadowy room. 'There's no air, not a breath,' she grumbled. 'I wish it would rain, even though the racket sounds like a crazy drummer on the roof.'

The intense humidity made sleep impossible that night, even though it was doubtful if the remorseless pattern of questions that reiterated through Venetia's brain would have allowed her to sleep. Supposing Claire didn't come back. What then? Would Jason just let her go? Della seemed so sure that Claire was still in love with him. But Della could be mistaken. Supposing Claire wanted her freedom, because she had other plans. What if those plans revolved round – *Simon Manville*?

The stifling dawn brought no answers, except the conviction that no matter how the impasse was resolved someone was going to be hurt.

Venetia's heart was heavy when she entered the office and listlessly removed the cover from the typewriter. With a defensive air of defiance Della had departed immediately after a very early breakfast for the Kinlay bungalow, and in her heart Venetia could not blame her. Faced with the same circumstances, would she herself have acted differently if it had been Simon who had been injured?

The morning dragged by, leaden minute by minute through an ever-increasing heat that even the whirring fans overhead seemed unable to keep at bay. Johnny breezed in, left a couple of analyses for her to decipher and copy, and departed with the announcement that he would be out of the base for the next three days. Mac came in and joined her for mid-morning coffee, and gestured at the skies, remarking that she would need her gumboots before the day was over.

'Or flippers,' she responded wryly from force of habit to Mac's inevitable gambit whenever the elements threatened.

She finished Johnny's reports soon after lunch and wondered what on earth she could find to occupy her time until four o'clock. Some days there was a rush of work, when people kept coming in, exchanging jocular or dour greetings, depending on their mood, and leaving a batch of work on her desk, but today was unusually slack, at the very time when she would have welcomed a crowded schedule to fill her thoughts to the exclusion of all else.

She plucked at the material where her blouse stuck to her damp skin and wiped a tissue over her face before she got up and wandered to the window. Outside, the lawns had a bleached, brassy tinge, like damp cropped straw, and the boys had stopped their desultory weeding of the scarlet flower beds that bordered the wide lawns.

There was a container which held disposable cups on the rack near the window. She took one out and filled it from the water cooler, and stood sipping the aerated drink. The tiny bubbles slowly subsided, and abruptly she drained the cup and tossed it into the basket. She might as well pack up now for the week-end. Her mouth drooped sadly. This was to have been the week-end spent with Simon, meeting his friends in Mortonstown. What were their names ...? Elaine and Roy ... But what did it matter? She wouldn't be meeting them now, or ever ...

Too listless to renew her lipstick, she flicked a comb through her hair and glanced round to make sure she had left everything tidy. Mac would switch off everything when he came back.

She opened the door and walked straight into Simon.

'Oh ...!' She fell back a pace, then averted her gaze and prepared to sidestep.

'Not so fast.' His hand closed round her arm. 'I want to talk to you.'

She looked at the taut forbidding lines of his jaw and felt a tremor of unease. 'What about?' she asked dully.

'As if you didn't know. How long has it gone on?'

'Has what gone on?' She stared at him. 'I don't know what you're talking about.'

'Listen, it's too late to play the innocent. I'm not going to stand by and see several lives botched up because a couple of empty-headed girls came to Africa to have six months' fun. Where's Jason? And your girl friend?'

'How should I know? I'm not their keeper.' She wrenched her arm out of his grip. 'Anyway, what's it to do with you?'

'Nothing. But somebody has to try and instil some sense round here. The fun's over. Understand?' His eyes were angry and there was air of suppressed violence in the way he towered over her, as though he were with difficulty restraining himself from actually shaking her to add physical emphasis to his words. 'Surely you must have seen this coming. You live with her. She's your closest friend. Or is she reticent with the girlish confidences?' he demanded scornfully. 'Maybe you didn't know she was quietly undermining the last stays in a marriage that's been shaky for the last three years!'

Sheer cold horror was rushing over Venetia as the bitter accusations were hammered at her. For a moment she was beyond speech, then anger drained the colour from her cheeks and lent power to a fierce defence of her friend.

'That's not true!' she stormed. 'You've no right to accuse her. You've only heard one side of it. Claire's side! You can't blame one person for everything. Least of all Della. She isn't that kind of a person. I know! And I'd believe her before I'd believe anybody else, especially Claire. *Or you!* But then I wouldn't expect you to have any understanding or mercy. Naturally you'll believe Claire. I'm not surprised, the way things are. Of course you'd—'

'What do you mean?' His eyes sparked angrily. He seized her by the shoulders. 'What do you mean by that? The way things are?'

'You should know!' she cried fiercely. 'Now let me go. I refuse to listen to any more of your – your beastly accusations!'

She wrenched herself out of his grasp and stared up at him with stormy, tear-drenched eyes. 'Let me remind you, Simon Manville! *You* had your fun as well! Well I hope you enjoyed it! Because I didn't!'

Before he could move to stop her she was running, blindly, before it was too late. Her breakdown, witnessed by Simon Manville, would be the final, most unbearable humiliation of all.

CHAPTER NINE

'Don't be so crazy, Ven. You can't possibly go off on your own. Not on the native bus.'

'And why shouldn't I go on the native bus? It'll get me there.'

'Yes, but it won't be exactly comfortable and the time-tables are erratic, to say the least.'

'I don't care about being late or early, as long as I get away.' Venetia stared despondently into space. 'If I have to stay here another day I'll go crazy.'

'I know how you feel, pet,' Della touched her shoulder sympathetically. 'I feel a bit like that myself.'

'Come with me,' Venetia said impulsively. 'I've got it all worked out. Mac is going to drive me as far as Noyali and drop me off just before he reaches the site. Then he's going to come round that way tonight and wait for me in the market place. Please come. It would be good for you to have a break.'

Della shook her head. 'I can't, pet, sorry.'

'I suppose you're going to Jason.'

'I am,' Della said calmly, 'when I've got through a few chores. Oh, don't look like that,' she added impatiently. 'Drew Chalmers is coming over as well. Though why I should worry, I don't know. Everybody thinks the worst, anyway.'

'I hate Simon Manville!' said Venetia in a low, vehement voice.

Della smiled sadly. 'You don't really. If he were to come to you and take back his words you'd fall into his arms and forgive him without a moment's hesitation.'

'I wouldn't,' she said bitterly. 'I never want to see him again as long as I live.'

'That's part of loving.' Della sighed and reached for her bathrobe. 'You'll get over it eventually, the same way as I'll get over Jason. Oh, God!' she exclaimed impatiently, 'let's not get maudlin. If you're determined to go into town will you bring me some shampoo and one of those giant tins of talc for everyday? Is there anything else . . .?' Della frowned. 'Oh, yes, I could do with—'

'Write it all down. I want a stack of stuff.' Venetia went to hunt out the gay straw basket Johnny had bought her – it seemed so long ago. 'I'd better take this.'

Mac hadn't forgotten his promise. He arrived in the Land Rover, and half an hour later deposited her at the bus terminus next to the market place. He leaned out and grinned. 'Don't stay out in the midday sun, mind, lassie. Get inside somewhere – the museum's about the coolest spot, and you'll need to be on the way back by nine, no later. Away ye go – and don't spend all your bawbees.'

The bus ride was as uncomfortable as Della had forecast. It was market day, and the small, bright blue bus was packed to suffocation with whole families and an assortment of livestock which added to the general tumult. Halfway on the journey the engine boiled as the vehicle finally reached the crest of a long winding gradient, and a quarter of an hour went by while the passengers waited for it to cool. No one seemed unduly disturbed and Venetia reflected that it was doubtless a regular occurrence, as was the hair-raising descent down the other side of the hill when the journey was resumed.

It was almost eleven when she got off the bus and thankfully stretched cramped limbs. Taking a mental note of landmarks and the direction she would have to take on her return at evening, she walked slowly along the Parade towards the main shopping precinct.

Later, she realized she should have left her shopping errands until the afternoon, but by then it was too late to regret the weight of the purchases she would have to tote around for the rest of the day. Long before the afternoon shadows began to lengthen she was weary and hot and uncomfortable. Her eyes ached with the glare of sun-baked pavements and her clothes stuck to her body as though they were plastered there. But no physical discomfort could equal the dreadful sense of loneliness she experienced after the moment she thought she saw Simon.

He was coming out of the airline office as she emerged from a book stall where she had bought the reading matter Della had requested. She was positive it was he. That coffee brown shirt open at the throat, the pale biscuit-coloured pants, the upright head and the dark glasses, that gesture to the rims as he replaced them when he emerged into the sunlight.

'Simon!' Hardly realizing she had cried the name aloud, she took off for the opposite side of the road, heedless of the screech of brakes from the big Chevrolet that swerved to avoid her headlong charge.

He had reached the corner, was turning along the intersection as she thrust her way among the dawdling shoppers, and was out of sight by the time her steps slowed, hurried again, and petered out. He had gone.

Sadly she walked on down the side street, still hoping for another glimpse of that particular combination of coffee and beige clothing a tall man who could make her forget the rest of the world.

The white buildings and the brilliant hues of the flowering shrubs beneath the palms blurred in a hot mist of tears. She crossed to the centre reservation and sat down on the edge of the low ornamental wall and almost

166

gave way to tears. Everyone seemed to have somewhere to go, some purpose, someone to meet. All she had was another three hours to kill, and after that . . .

The streets were becoming less crowded now. People were making their diverse ways to home, hotels, or friends. The European shops were closing, and the boys were appearing with the evening editions. On impulse she bought a paper and from it found inspiration: the cinema. The answer to loneliness and aching lassitude.

But the cinema was African. Even though it was new and streamlined, it was roofless, and the evening showing did not begin until eight o'clock. Venetia turned away and the first rumble of the storm shuddered in the heavens.

This was all she needed to complete a disastrous day!

From an open-fronted soda bar, she watched the streets empty and the rivulets become a river in the road. The skies darkened as though it was night, and the lightning contended in eerie brilliance with the winking neon of a Schweppes sign at the other side of the road. Why did familiar things only serve to emphasize the alienness of their settings? she wondered.

She bought another Tropical Glory and lit another cigarette, wondering how much longer she was to be marooned. For the first time she experienced a tremor of unease. Normally she was not unduly frightened of storms, but the intensity of a tropical storm was unnerving when she was so far from home. Supposing it didn't abate soon. She thought of the journey earlier in the day and tried to imagine it in the darkness, over those long miles of rough track, those nightmare hills and the drop down into the bush . . . in a storm like this . . .

Abruptly she pushed the half full glass aside and slid off her stool. It was time she got back to the bus station.

The newspaper kept her head and shoulders dry for approximately a couple of minutes. She shoved the sodden grey pulp into a litter bin and surrendered herself to the elements – and fate. With numb foreboding she knew they had not yet done with her, knew that all that motley crowd of fellow passengers this morning would not be stranded as she was, knew what the man in the car was going to say when he drew to a halt and looked curiously at her from the shelter of the interior. He was oldish, with an unhealthy yellow skin and a balding head, and his accent had a rough twang she couldn't place.

He said: 'You've had it, miss. They don't run 'em out into the bush when it's like this. Bogged to the axles they'd be. From the Dam site, you say? Long way out, aren't you, miss? You'd best stay overnight. Hop in, I'm passing the Africa.'

'No, thanks.' She took a step back. She did not like him – and how could she present herself at any hotel like this? 'I've got friends,' she mumbled. 'There's a booth over there. I'll phone . . . Good night – thank you.' Before he could repeat his offer she scurried away into the darkness.

The light bulb was missing in the booth, but somehow she managed to sort out the necessary coins and the operator's number. Then the thought struck her: which number did she ask for? The Admin. office would be closed for the night by now, and the storm would have stopped all work at the site. Would anybody be there? But Mac would wait. He knew she was here . . .

It was a long time before she could believe the guttural statement that rang in her ears long after an impatient operator cut off the other end of the line. It couldn't be! The line couldn't be down. It— Desperate now, she tried again.

'*The Noyali line is out of order, caller!*'

Unaware that she was trembling as though with an ague, she stared at the mute receiver and tried to force her mind to think. What on earth was she going to do? No transport, and no means of communication with the people who could help her. She did not doubt for one moment that any of them would set off immediately, no matter how bad the storm, if only she could get through. There was nothing else for it; she would have to find a hotel . . .

'Are you going to be in there all night, miss?'

The booth door opened and a craggy, bad-tempered face looked at her indignantly. Hardly seeing the man, she said dully, 'The line's out of order.'

'Oh, Gawd, no! Here, let me see.' He crowded in beside her and snatched up the phone, his mouth twitching impatiently as he waited. 'Were you trying for a local number?'

'The Noyali line's down,' she repeated.

'Oh, Gawd,' he said again. 'That's bleedin' well torn it.'

Dimly she sensed that she was not the only one to whom the storm spelled trouble. 'Are you stranded as well?' she asked.

'No – but my wife's on her own and she's terrified of storms. She'll be in a screaming tizzy by now. I wanted to check that she's okay and warn her I'll be hours yet.' He gave her a jerky glance. 'Did you say you were stranded?'

'Yes.' She started to explain and he cut her short. 'You were mad. You'll never get back to Noyali tonight.' For a moment he stared from under grizzled sandy brows and some of the sharpness left his expression. He said abruptly:

'Listen, I'm a planter. My place is out on the far side of

Noyali. I'll give you a lift that far if it's any help. Can't promise any farther, but we could put you up for the night, or you can phone from our place and maybe somebody can come out and pick you up.'

She hesitated, sudden doubt obvious in the shadowed eyes searching the stranger's rugged features. He glanced at his watch and thrust the booth door open. 'Now make your mind up. I can't stand here all night.'

'I – I—' She looked out uncertainly at the storm tossed night and tightened her grip on her bag. 'It's very kind of you, but I—'

'Listen, kid, you'll have to take me on trust. My name's Jed Clavering. I'm fifty-five. I've three kids back home all older than you look, and I'm too bleedin' tired for fun and games. All I want is to get to hell out of this and back to my wife.'

'I – I'm sorry. I didn't mean . . . I'd be very grateful if you'd take me. You see I haven't anything with me to go to a hotel and stay—'

But he had already turned away, gesturing towards the big solid shape of the estate wagon looming by the kerb. It smelled of oil and stale fruit and various other odours she couldn't define, but it was transport and it was going to get her somewhere within reach of home. And even Jed Clavering's brusqueness was preferable to facing the night alone.

He gave a desultory swipe at the smeary windscreen and switched on wiper-blades that twitched and slid wheezily in slow jerky half-moon sweeps. 'There's an oilskin in the back there,' he gestured, 'you can shove it round you if you turn cold.'

'Thank you – I'm warm enough just now,' she said politely.

'You look half drowned to me.' He put the vehicle into

motion, steering with one big roughened hand while with the other he fumbled for a cheroot and lit it, adding a pungent odour that made the others somewhat less noticeable.

'Like a tot?' he said as an afterthought. 'There's a flask under there somewhere.'

She saw the end of the battered, blackened flask protruding from a jumble of rags, tattered papers, a spanner and what looked suspiciously like a gun. Looking at its dull metallic snout, she said politely: 'No, thank you – I just had three Tropical Glories while I was waiting for the rain to stop.'

'Blow you out, those things,' he grunted, and lapsed into silence.

That journey would always remain in Venetia's memory for the strange air of unreality it held. She suspected the estate wagon had seen better days, and once the reasonably smooth road outside the capital was left behind the vehicle began to betray its protests at the punishment under-wheel. The springs groaned, and Venetia got the impression that every so often an unsuspected piledriver lurked under her seat and launched into operation, sending dull shock waves up her spine. The storm seemed to have slightly lessened in intensity, which was one blessing, she reflected wryly, shifting a little to one side to give one half of her frame a respite from the piledriving vibrations. It was like a long plane flight, she thought; when this was over she would still feel the throb and hear the noise of the engine.

Jed Clavering alternated between spells of silence and bouts of garrulous confidences about his family. None of his children had the slightest inclination to join their parents. The eldest daughter was married to a garage mechanic in Hitchin and had been saving up ever since her wedding to come out to spend a holiday with her parents, but the first baby had postponed this plan, and the second baby had pushed it further back into the realm of later – 'when we get turned round and the kids are a bit older'; no doubt a third baby would arrive and some time would become never ... The youngest daughter cherished ambitions to be an actress. 'Don't know where she gets it from,' said Jed Clavering. 'She was born out here, never set eyes on a pantomime until she went home to her gran and started school. Turned out a real smasher, she has. Don't know where she gets it from,' he added. 'I'm no oil painting, and Bessie's the real homely type.'

But it was his son who worried Jed. 'Just drifts,' he said sadly, changing down for another grind uphill. 'Had him here for six months and he was off again. Nine jobs since he finished at tech. Now he's bumming across Persia with another couple of scruffy, long-haired tykes.'

He lit another cheroot and lapsed back into morose silence.

Venetia sighed and reflected on the little world she had entered which was peopled with individuals she was never likely to meet or hear of again. Yet at the moment she felt close to them, their hopes, fears and conflicts helped to keep at bay her own hopeless despair. Useless to tell herself that Simon Manville wasn't worth an ounce of heartache. Useless to try to console herself with the stricture that a man who could leap to conclusions and bracket her in the accusations he had flung at Della was basically devoid of either understanding or compassion. Her heart would hear none of it; it persisted in remembering the things she wanted to forget. A man's mouth quirking at one corner as he said: *'That was for the practice run – it might improve if you let it.'* The audacious challenge in grey eyes over a waxen pink blossom thrust into the valley of her breats ... *You're beginning to grow up, little one.'* ... *'But it's the inshine girls men marry ...'* Oh, Simon! She *had* to stop torturing herself with bitter hopeless longings for what could never be. Realize the truth; it was all just a flip of a coin! Just fun and—

A violent jerk brought her back to the black night, the fusillade of the torrent against the windscreen, and the great pool of red-cocoa slime reflecting the headlamps. Jed Clavering swore and inched forward into the viscous mass. It swirled against the wheels, impeding, reluctantly coagulating into the vacuum they left with nauseous, glutinous squelches.

Instinctively she drew her feet beneath her, almost expecting to see the ominous pools oozing up through the floor of the vehicle. With the despair of fatalism she wondered if this was to be the final catastrophe; to be bogged down in mud in the heart of the forest. Wisely she kept her fear to herself; Jed Clavering had enough to worry about driving through it, without feminine panic to add to his troubles.

It seemed hours before the surface of the track loomed ahead in the watery glare of the lamps. Muddy and raddled with pools, but at least the ruts were discernible, she noticed, heaving a sigh of relief.

But there was no sigh of relief from her companion.

Venetia did not know a great deal about mechanics, but she recognized an engine in trouble. The bumpiest track in the world didn't make an engine cough and splutter as though about to spew out its guts.

She said in a whisper that shook slightly: 'Have we very far to go?'

'Far enough,' he said grimly. 'With a bit of luck we'll make it.'

She could only huddle back and pray for that bit of luck. The ironical thought came and she almost laughed aloud; Jed Clavering didn't know he had a gremlin for a passenger. It wasn't her day, and her presence certainly wouldn't help his along. She glanced at her watch and stifled a gasp of dismay. It was long after ten. Mac would have given her up long since. Then, as though her sigh were the signal, the vehicle stopped.

'Sorry, kid. We've had it.' Jed Clavering reached for the flask, swallowed a quick mouthful, and replaced the cap. 'I thought she wasn't going to make that last mile.'

Venetia looked at him wordlessly. What difference did the last mile make? They were stranded just the same, whether here or fifty miles away. Then alarm widened her eyes as she saw him reaching into the back and pulling out the oilskin. Surely he wasn't going to suggest walking, in *this*! Then logic prevailed and she realized he was going to investigate the damage. But she was wrong on both counts. The oilskin in an untidy bunch over his arm, he turned to her and said brusquely: 'Are you as nervy as my missus?'

'I – I don't know,' she faltered. 'Why?'

'Because you've two choices. You can stay behind while I walk the rest of the way and come back in the old horse, or you can come with me?'

With difficulty she repressed a groan. Neither of these alternatives appealed in the least, in fact, they appalled.

'If you're wise you'll stay put. To be honest, kid, I don't think you'll make it.'

'How far is it?' she whispered.

He shrugged. 'About four miles.'

She looked at the night, at the mudbath of a track, the glistening black of the undergrowth and the sombre trees under the dark veil of rain, and her heart quailed.

She knew when she was beaten. 'I'll wait,' she said, 'but . . .'

'But what?'

'How long will you be?'

He shrugged again. 'A couple of hours at the most. Maybe less. It ain't exactly a running track, you know.'

She nodded, and to her surprise he thrust the oilskin at her. 'You'd best put that on till you get inside.'

'Inside?' She stared.

He clapped at his head. 'You don't know the area, do you? There's an old shack just round this bend. Used to be part of the old estate before we rebuilt five years ago. It ain't exactly a home from home, but at least it'll be dry and there's a stove you can light and dry yourself out.'

Once again Venetia surrendered herself up to the fates. Some time it would end, and she would be back in sane surroundings among faces she knew, and a recognizable pattern would begin to re-form. She wriggled into the clammy oilskin and collected her limp, rain-soaked possessions together, then stepped out reluctantly into the morass.

Jed Clavering was kindly enough in his rough brusque way. He kept a firm steadying grip on her arm until he had steered her the mercifully short distance to the small, ramshackle building set in a small clearing just off the track.

The door creaked dismally as he pushed it open, and the musty smell of mildew stirred in the dank interior. There was little inside, an old bicycle resting against one wall, a couple of packing cases and a chair with a broken leg, an old-fashioned hump-backed trunk over which the ghostly film of mould had crept. Jed Clavering swung the powerful light of a heavy torch around the floor and Venetia had a sudden horrified suspicion that an army of cockroaches had fled precipitately from this unexpected intrusion. But Jed was not looking for 'roaches. He upturned the packing cases, cast a searching glance well into corners, and announced: 'Okay – no unwelcome company. The only place might be the stove pipe and the smoke will soon do the trick.'

With a shudder she realized he meant snakes! Silently she watched while he removed an ancient kettle from the top of the stove and provided fuel by the crude but effective means of putting his foot through one of the packing cases. A rag smeared with petrol started it crackling and he clamped the lid back on the stove.

'It won't burn long, but it'll be warm enough to dry you out. I'll leave the door open behind the screen in case you steam alive, and I'll leave the torch. You'll be okay if you don't wander abroad and I'll be back as sharp as I can. So long!'

The sounds of his steps diminished and faded into the dull sullen drum of the rain on the roof. After a while even that became blunted and part of the heavy lifeless stillness inside the shack. She took off her skirt and blouse and spread them over the stove, uncaring now of their being further soiled, and huddled in the oilskin for the short time they took to dry. They felt limp and unpleasant when she donned them again, and the sheer need to fill the leaden minutes made her comb and rub at her hair until the tendrils began to fluff out again and curl in their soft framing cap of gold about her head.

Every two or three minutes she looked at her watch and made sure it hadn't stopped. Surely more than half an hour had elapsed since Jed Clavering had gone. She spread the oilskin on top of the other packing case and gingerly tested her weight on it before she extracted Della's magazines from her basket and slowly turned the pages . . .

Velvet was back for evening wear this coming winter. Waistlines would rise and shiny fabrics were out. . . Had Jed Clavering reached home yet? Supposing he got stuck coming back. A fallen tree across the track . . . The 'in' place for winter sunshine was Babul – but only if one stayed at a caravanserai – and the newest vogue in interior design was the Roman look . . .

A flicker of unearthly light and a shattering roar of thunder brought her to rigid immobility. The magazine slipped from her hands and fell to the floor as she waited for this fresh tumult to subside in the heavens. The wind was increasing, its force carrying moisture through the mesh of the screen, and she could sense the trail of its passage through leaf and branch.

The torch light seemed dimmer, and another thunder-clap set free the demons of panic. Jed Clavering wasn't coming back. Something had happened. His wife was ill. He couldn't get back. Something had happened to *him*! She was stuck here in a shack – she didn't know where – and nobody knew where she was, and she was more frightened than she had ever been, ever . . . It was long after midnight and she hadn't eaten since teatime, but if a banquet were spread out before her she wouldn't be able to eat a morsel.

The wind was battering against the screen as though with the fists of a giant invader, and it seemed that all the furies of hell had been loosed outside. Jed Clavering would never get back through all this; no one could fight these elemental forces – unless they were equipped with a tank, she thought with rising hysteria.

For what seemed an aeon she huddled there, the oil-skin drawn over her head to try to shut out the clamour and her fear, while the storm raged with renewed fury.

If only the light held out! If the precious glow faded she couldn't bear any more. She should conserve it, turn the thing at the top that changed the focus ... perhaps it would last a bit longer ... With trembling fingers she twisted the top of the heavy, old-fashioned torch and the beam flickered and went out altogether. At the moment of her cry another sound penetrated the roar outside.

A car klaxon. Jed Clavering was back. Thank heaven! The torch rolled across the floor and she blundered towards the door. Her hands could not locate the catch quickly enough, and a sob of desperation escaped her as she found it and wrestled with its stiffness. It gave suddenly and the force of the wind raged into the shack, bringing the door crashing back into her. Wet flurries of leaves and debris swept in a rough clammy tide against her legs as she stumbled out on to the tiny ramshackle verandah fronting the building.

For an instant she could see nothing except wild angry blackness, then a flash of eerie electric blue illuminated the swaying silhouettes of the trees and the glistening brown quagmire of the track. A man was coming towards her, his head bent as he braced himself against the force of the tempest.

The glare died and the figure dissolved into the darkness, then she saw the ghostly glisten of his waterproof as it billowed out and flapped like the wings of some great preying bird. Thick panic clogged Venetia's throat. This wasn't Jed Clavering!

Jed Clavering was small and thin and wiry. This was someone else – *something* else! She stepped back, straight on to the fallen torch, and cried aloud with fright before she realized what it was and bent to grab it. Her nerveless fingers twisted it and shook it desperately. Why wouldn't it light? Then another unearthly blue glow filmed the scene. She saw the man stop, saw his arm go up, and at last – his face.

Wild laughter bubbled up in her. She had rubbed the lamp and the genie had come. It was magic, it couldn't be true! But she began to run . . .

CHAPTER TEN

'STEADY on, little one, it's only a storm – you're safe now.'

His voice sounded a long way away, its nuances carried above her head on the wings of the wind. She was still unsure if it was all real, if it was really Simon magically materialized out of the night or some cruel incantation born of the storm and the witchery of the forest. If she moved or spoke the next flash of lightning would dissolve the fantasy, restore the emptiness of the night ... With the feverish thought she felt the hand cradling her head cease its consoling ruffling caress.

'This is all very satisfying – but we're going to drown on our feet any minute.'

A great sigh shuddered through her. He *was* real; no sorcery could emulate that particular note of tender irony, or the hard, heaven-sent strength of him against which the wind and the rain and the force of her own fervent relief had pasted her with an efficiency any billposter would have admired.

Awkwardly she disengaged herself and frantically took refuge in the babble of normality. 'Yes, we'd better go ... where've you left the car? ... I'll get my things ... they're in there ...'

But he was following her into the shack, slamming the door shut behind him, shaking and dashing the moisture off his dark hair. 'I'm afraid we'll have to ride it out for a little while. It must abate soon.'

He was moving in the darkness and she could hear the rustling sounds of him shaking his waterproof and a moment later a light sprang from his hand and played round the drab interior, finally coming to rest on her white face.

'Still scared, little one? Cheer up, it'll soon be over.'

'Is – is it really you?' she faltered, still not completely convinced. 'I'm not dreaming?'

'I don't know about your dreams, but I'm real enough.' He moved forward, held his hand over the stove and then draped the waterproof over the top. 'God, what a night!' Suddenly he laughed. 'Did you think I was a ghost?'

'No – yes – that is, I couldn't believe it was you. How did you know?'

'It's quite a story.' He was prowling round the shack, finally coming to the packing case and testing its solidity before he sat on the edge. 'Mac was worried sick about you when you didn't arrive at the appointed place. He waited for a while, then decided you must have stayed overnight in town. But your friend wasn't very happy about it, in fact she was going to set off for Noyali to see if you'd turned up. As we couldn't persuade her that it was highly unlikely I drove along there myself to make sure. Naturally there was no sign of you, and I'd probably have given up and gone back if I hadn't run into Harper and three of his cronies. They'd been on the razzle in town, and while I knew it was improbable that they'd seen anything of you I asked just the same.'

Simon paused to get out his cigarettes, and an expression of disgust crossed his face. 'They were pretty well stoned, and when they told me that the native bus was stuck on the track down by the boundary of the Shearwater place I began to get worried. I gathered it was deserted, and there was no sign of anybody being hurt, but I wondered what had become of you if you'd been on it. So,' he shrugged, 'there was nothing else to do but to set out and look for you. I'll admit I didn't relish the thought of driving to town in this, but it was the only way to set our minds at rest.'

'But you'd never find anyone at that time of night,' she said, 'I mean, if I had stayed there overnight.'

He smiled faintly. 'There are only two principal hotels to check on, and a couple of smaller places you might have picked on. And Della assured me you didn't know a soul there to whom you might have gone for the night. However, about four miles back I met Jed Clavering. A man on foot at this time of night is obviously in trouble, so naturally I stopped, and the rest should be obvious. I've never seen Jed look so happy as when he realized he didn't have to turn out again to rescue you.'

After a pause she said slowly: 'Would you really have gone all the way to Mortonstown, in this, to try and find me?'

'Of course.' His tone was quite flat. 'I'd be a callous individual if I'd just ignored all the possibilities that might have happened. Quite honestly, little one, the thought of you wandering round alone in a tropical storm at night isn't exactly conducive to anyone's peace of mind, least of all mine.'

'Oh.' She couldn't think of anything more intelligent to say at that precise moment.

'Why on earth didn't you say you wanted transport into town, anyway?' he demanded suddenly. 'I'd have taken you with me – and got you back safely.'

For a moment she couldn't respond, unable to voice a suitable retort to the question and the inevitable reaction it evoked. At last she said. 'After last night I – I didn't think of asking you. Anyway, you weren't going to town, not that I knew of, and I couldn't ask you to, especially for me.' Aware of becoming slightly confused, she added firmly: 'It didn't occur to me.'

'After last night?' he said dryly. 'Okay, we'll leave that for the moment. But as it happens, I did run through to town today.'

'Then I *did* see you!' The words were out before she could check them, and she added more slowly, 'I saw you this afternoon.'

'Then why didn't you say something?' he exclaimed. 'I certainly didn't see you – if I had, all this wouldn't have happened.' He raised his hands. 'You mean you stood and watched me and kept doggo?'

'No!' she cried, indignation overcoming caution. 'I shouted, but you didn't hear. If you must know, I chased you all the way down the Parade.'

'The Parade?' He frowned.

'Yes, you were coming out of the airline office and you turned down a side road and I lost sight of you.' She paused. 'You didn't hear me.'

To her surprise he was suddenly laughing. 'I wouldn't be likely to hear you, either, considering I was never within a mile of the Parade at any time today.'

'You mean . . .' Dismay swept over her face. 'You mean you – I—'

'I don't know who it was you pursued down the Parade, but perhaps it's as well you didn't catch him. And what was this desirable prey like?'

'It's not funny. He had a shirt exactly the same as that dark brown one of yours, and he was tall and dark and—'

'Handsome?' Simon said sardonically. 'Go on, say it. No one's ever said I was handsome before. How else did this paragon resemble me?'

'He had dark glasses, and he twitched them when he put them on, just like you do sometimes, and—' She stopped, her mouth starting to quiver as she recalled the sheer misery of those moments when loneliness had enclosed her amid the colour and the bustle of the sunlit town. 'It's not funny,' she repeated soberly.

'No, it isn't.' His own expression had sobered. He held out his arms. 'Come here, and I'll say I'm sorry.'

She looked at the etched shadows of his features and shook her head. 'You don't need to. It was silly, anyway.'

'Was it? Come here.'

'No.' Nevertheless, she moved a step forward, and he caught her hands, drawing her towards him until she stood pressed against his knees.

He looked up at the small set face just a little way above the level of his eyes. 'Did you really chase a total stranger thinking it was me?'

'Of course I did. If you think I'm making it up I – I wish I'd never told you.'

'I'm very glad you did. But you're cold.' He brought her hands together between his own. 'I hope you haven't got a chill. By the way, how long since you ate?' he asked with disconcerting suddenness.

'So long I've forgotten.' She looked down at the strong hands and wished she could summon the willpower to break their disturbing contact.

But the next moment this difficult effort was unnecessary. Simon loosed his grasp and stood up. 'How far away is Jed's jalopy?'

'Not very far – a few yards back,' she said. 'Why?'

'Did he lock it?'

'I think so, but why? You're not thinking of—?'

'No.' He was already seizing his waterproof and shrugging into it. 'I should say it's a certainty that Jed has a load of provisions in the back. In an emergency like this I'm sure he wouldn't object to our raiding them. There might be something to stay the pangs for an hour or so.'

The wild gusts raged into the shack as he opened the door, obviously with the intention of going forth into the night. Sudden, unreasoning panic pervaded Venetia and galvanized her into action. 'No!' she rushed to the door. 'No, don't go out there. I'm not really hungry! It doesn't matter. Don't bother, Simon. It—'

'But it does. It'll only take me a few minutes.'

Not realizing she had caught at his arm, she looked at him with imploring eyes, unable to voice the nameless fears of what might happen if he went out into the storm and out of her sight, and knowing only that she couldn't bear to be left alone again. 'There's a great swamp on the track,' she said desperately. 'It's flooded. You might—'

'I mightn't.' Calmly he faced her, put his hands on each side of her head and touched his lips to her brow. 'Nothing will happen to me and I intend to make sure nothing's going to happen to you. Now sit down like a good girl' – again that light pressure of lips against her forehead – 'and wait until I break into poor Jed Clavering's car for something to bring the colour back into those pale cheeks.'

His hands fell away and at last something snapped in Venetia. She turned blindly in the doorway and cried: 'Well, don't! I don't want anything – except to get out of here, and you to stop being so kind and – and considerate one moment, and – and blaming me for everything the next.' Her voice choked and she found to her horror that she was beginning to tremble. 'I know it's been a hell of a nuisance for you having to drag yourself out here, but you didn't have to, I'd have got back eventually, so stop being so – gentle when you know you don't mean it.'

There was a moment of painful silence and a perceptible tautness in the atmosphere. Then Simon said coolly, 'But I happen to mean it. And I shall go on being *just* kind one moment and blaming you the next – until *you* stop being afraid of loving me.'

She raised a startled, bewildered face and sought to make sense of this calm, peremptory announcement. But it wouldn't make sense, except the painful truth she'd been trying to deny in every waking moment since she'd been drawn unwillingly into Simon Manville's orbit.

'When are you going to stop fighting me?' he asked at last when it was plain she was going to make no response. 'It was never my idea of loving.'

'I don't know what your idea of loving is,' she said in an unsteady whisper, 'but I don't think it's anything like mine.'

'No?' There was a certain grimness of purpose in the step he took forward. 'I think it's time we found out. This isn't exactly my idea of a romantic spot for the job, but I'm damned if I'm going to wait any longer to discover whether an infuriating little minx who doesn't seem to know her own heart has any feeling for mine.' His arms pinioned round her and, now, kindness would be the last word to describe aptly the emotion Simon was unleashing. Crushed in that fierce embrace, she barely heard the whispered: *'When are you going to grow up?'* before the mouth voicing the despairing plea effectively silenced any response she might have made.

When at last he drew back she was beyond either response or protest. She leaned weakly against him and waited until the world came back – if it ever would – and wondered how she had ever existed before Simon came.

'Well, have you found *your* answer?' he said softly.

'You're being cruel now,' she murmured against his chest.

'You said you didn't want me to be kind. Oh, darling, you'll have to get used to my teasing you.' His arms drew her even closer and he rubbed his cheek against her hair. 'I can't help it, and it seems the only way I ever winkle an answer out of you.'

'You've got your own answering to do first.' Gaining

186

confidence, she wriggled her arms through the annoying barriers of waterproof folds and found the deep satisfaction of enclosing Simon's broad muscular back within her clasp. 'Go on, talk.'

'I've always found actions far more expressive than words,' he said resignedly, 'but I know women like to hear these things and have it all down in black and white. Very well, I'll give your answer. You'll have to say yes in any case, so why waste any more time?'

'Yes to what?' She was smiling now.

'Seeing this is the second night we've spent together – there can't be much of this one left – we'll have to get married. No woman ever compromised me and got away with it.'

'I don't think I want to try.' She gave a blissful sigh and looked up into his face, meeting a gaze that set her heart surging again in a wild, tempestuous rhythm. The last little doubt vanished and she knew she need seek no further assurances of his love for her.

A long while later she stirred, reluctantly allowing all the hovering influences of the other part of her life to come back into this new joyous existence. 'It doesn't seem fair to have so much happiness,' she sighed, 'while others . . . Simon . . . ?'

'Yes, my little one?'

'Della isn't really an adventuress or anything. Try not to misjudge her, she's terribly worried about Jason and Claire.'

'Oh, yes.' Simon put her from him and moved out on to the verandah, glancing up at the night sky. 'The storm's over – did you realize?'

'No.' She followed him, savouring the cool, rain-washed sweetness of the storm's aftermath. 'What were you going to say?'

'I haven't told you today's news. Come on, let's get out of this dump. Where's your stuff?'

'Here – I just had the basket and my bag. I'll leave Jed's oilskin here, shall I? He can pick it up when he comes back for his – Simon! What are you doing?'

'Carrying you – the mud's about two feet thick by the look of it. Any objections?'

'Not if your muscles haven't. But don't try to drop me like you once did!'

'From the way your paws are clamped round me there's no fear of that,' he said dryly, picking his way carefully over the branch-strewn morass and apparently oblivious of the steady bumping of her basket against his back. 'Claire's had second thoughts.'

'Is she coming back?'

'I brought her back this afternoon.' He set his burden down and kept one arm round her waist while he sorted out his car keys. 'Whether they make a go of it this time is in the lap of the gods. I've done my part towards it.'

'I thought she had you in line at one time.' Venetia settled herself down and sighed for the joy of being able to confide the fears which had seemed so real such a short time ago. 'And you always seemed to take her side,' she added, with a sidelong glance to see how *that* was received.

'Somebody had to take her side. I know you two didn't hit it off with her, but she hadn't much to be happy about and no one could blame her for being jealous of Della.'

'Poor Della!' Venetia sighed. 'I wish there was some other way, that it hadn't happened like this. She didn't want it to happen this way. She's worked with Jason for so long. Now . . . I know she won't stay once this contract is completed.'

'I don't think you should worry too much about her.'

Simon touched her hand before he set the car into motion. 'I know you're fond of her, but she's a great deal wiser and less emotional than you are. She'll get over Jason sooner than you imagine and somebody will come along who'll make her forget all this career business.'

'Yes ...' Venetia lapsed into silence and mused pensively over Simon's words. For the first time she began to wonder if Della was as wise as she had always believed. Della had warned her against falling in love at all – as though anyone could avoid the onslaught of that overwhelming state of heart! She had warned against Simon, yet she had been unable to see the danger inherent in her own relationship with Jason. Poor Della had proved as vulnerable as the next when one certain man decided to turn on his charm, and that man hadn't been free. She sighed again, still wishing she could share all her own wonderful new-found happiness, then became aware of the car stopping.

They were at the point of the track from where the great dam was visible and she gave a small exclamation. She had never seen it during the hours of darkness, and now, its huge white curve brilliant in the floodlights that illuminated the work which went on ceaselessly, it held a strange striking grandeur against the deep velvet blue of the sky and the dark outline of the hills beyond.

Simon drew her into the curve of his arm and for a while they were silent, reflecting on the alien beauty of man's achievement in the heart of pagan nature. Presently Simon turned to her, and she felt a small metallic disc slide into her palm.

She looked down at it. 'What's this? It – it's a penny!'

He nodded. 'It's a very special penny. It's the penny I tossed to win you from Johnny.'

'Oh . . .'

'If you turn it over – here, hold it under the light from the dash – it might mean something. I don't know.' He turned away, apparently losing interest.

Slowly she turned it over, still puzzled, then comprehension came with blinding force. 'But it's a double-headed penny! It's the same on both sides.' She looked up. 'Oh, Simon, you villain! This is the penny you spun for me?'

'The very one – I had to make sure of you.'

'Even then – before you ever knew me?'

He nodded, and at last she was convinced. 'Can I have it – to keep?' she asked, closing the coin in her hand as though it were something very precious.

'As long as you remember who goes with it.' He reached for her, and with a little cry she surrendered herself joyously into his keeping, unashamedly revelling in the demand of his mouth and arms. At last he drew back and said rather unsteadily: 'You *are* growing up fast, little one – too fast. A second night spent with you without the magic circle isn't such a good idea, after all.'

He caressed the slender finger that would not be ringless much longer, then kissed it gently and sighed as her fingers clung and returned his caress. 'Come on, home,' he said gruffly.

She looked into the eyes that mirrored her own emotion, and wished passionately she could find the words with which perfectly to convey all the things she wanted to say. But the desired phrases would not shape themselves and she gave a soft little murmur and burrowed tightly against him. She felt the sigh of his indrawn breath against her as he drew her close and said softly: 'Now what, little one?'

'Nothing, Simon . . . I just love you.'

Mills & Boon Classics

The very best of Mills & Boon
romances, brought back for those of you
who missed reading them when they
were first published.

There are three other Classics for you to collect this
March

A SAVAGE BEAUTY
by Anne Mather

The disturbing Miguel Salvaje married Emma Seaton against
her will and bore her back to Mexico as his wife. There was a
state of perpetual conflict between them, and to make
matters worse Emma found there was another woman sharing
the house with her and her new husband ...

RING OF JADE
by Margaret Way

On the magical tropical island, Brockway's Folly, in the Great
Barrier Reef, Claire met two men — David who needed her
and Adam who didn't. Claire had come to the island to
escape her emotions — but instead she found them threatening
to overwhelm her completely.

LUCIFER'S ANGEL
by Violet Winspear

When Fay, young and inexperienced, married a sophisticated
film director, and was swept into the brittle, shallow social
whirl of Hollywood, she soon discovered that all too often
there is heartache behind the glitter.

Mills & Boon Classics

The very best of Mills & Boon
romances, brought back for those of
you who missed reading them
when they were first published.

in
April
we bring back the following four
great romantic titles.

CINDERELLA IN MINK
by Roberta Leigh

Nicola Rosten was used to the flattery and deference accorded
to a very wealthy woman. Yet Barnaby Grayson mistook her
for a down-and-out and set her to work in the kitchen!

MASTER OF SARAMANCA
by Mary Wibberley

Gavin Grant was arrogant and overbearing, thought Jane, and
she hadn't ever disliked anyone quite so much. Yet . . .

NO GENTLE POSSESSION
by Anne Mather

After seven years, Alexis Whitney was returning to Karen's
small town. It was possible that he might not even remember
her — but Karen hoped desperately that he did.

A SONG BEGINS
by Mary Burchell

When Anthea began her training with the celebrated operatic
conductor, Oscar Warrender, she felt her dreams were coming
true — but would she be tough enough to work under such an
exacting taskmaster?

If you have difficulty in obtaining any of these books through
your local paperback retailer, write to:

Mills & Boon Reader Service
P.O. Box 236, Thornton Road, Croydon, Surrey, CR9 3RU.